6.00
12/63

THE WICKED ONE

.

Also by Mollie Hunter:

The Stronghold
(awarded the Carnegie Medal 1975)
The Haunted Mountain
A Stranger Came Ashore
A Sound of Chariots
The Ghosts of Glencoe
A Pistol in Greenyards
The Lothian Run
The Thirteenth Member
The Walking Stones
The Kelpie's Pearls
Talent Is Not Enough
Mollie Hunter on Writing for Children

MOLLIE HUNTER

THE
WICKED
ONE

A Story of Suspense

HARPER & ROW, PUBLISHERS
New York, Hagerstown, San Francisco, London

THE WICKED ONE

Copyright © 1977 by Maureen Mollie Hunter McIlwraith

FIRST AMERICAN EDITION

Library of Congress Cataloging in Publication Data
McIlwraith, Maureen Mollie Hunter McVeigh, date
    The wicked one.

    SUMMARY: Incessantly tormented by the Grollican, a
creature of the Otherworld, Colin Grant and his family
flee to America from their native Highlands of Scotland.
    [1. Scotland—Fiction]   I. Title.
PZ7.M18543Wi   [Fic]   76-41515
ISBN 0-06-022647-1
ISBN 0-06-022648-X lib. bdg.

Contents

THE WICKED ONE

1 In the Forest

THERE WAS this man, it seems, who was troubled by one of those Otherworld creatures that can be seen or not seen, just as they choose. "The Grollican" is what they call this creature, but very often it is also known as "the wicked one", and the man who had the misfortune to be troubled by it was called Colin Grant.

It was in the Highlands of Scotland that this happened, in the kind of mountain valley which the people of these parts call a glen. This, they say, is where Colin Grant had his home; and according to all accounts, too, he was a very decent sort of a fellow. Also, he was handsome enough, although rather small in build. He was very strong for his size, however, and he worked as a forester among the miles of fir trees which cover the slopes of that glen; but like the rest of the people there at that time, he also had the few acres of farming land they call a croft.

When times were slack in the forestry, Colin worked this croft himself. When he was too busy for that, his family had to take care of it; but there was no problem there because his wife, Anna, had a good head on her shoulders. Furthermore, he and Anna had three sons, a young boy called Ian, and two older twin brothers named Hugh and Hector. Ian, as it happened, had suffered the bad luck of being born with a crooked shoulder, which meant he was not fitted for any really hard work; but even so, he had a good way with animals, while the twins were great strapping lads, taller than Colin himself. And thus, between them all, they managed to make a reasonable living.

They got on well together as a family, too—although Colin had to admit to one very serious fault in his nature. He had an extremely fiery temper; and it was this very fault that led to all the trouble, because the sort of man the Grollican picks on is always just like Colin—a decent man working hard at his job, yet still a man whose quick temper can make him his own worst enemy.

It was a piece of very bad luck for Colin, also, that he happened to be a forester to trade, since one thing that the Grollican greatly enjoys is lurking about in the gloom of a fir forest, and this was how it came to notice him in the first place. Or so they say, anyway, and certainly it was in the forest that Colin had his first experience of the wicked one.

The time it happened, it seems, was in the mouth of the night —which is the way they have there of describing the twilight that happens before dark. Colin had just finished his day's work and was walking home with his forester's axe over his shoulder, when he glimpsed something large and greyish flitting silently through the trees to his left.

"A deer!" thought he, because the ground in these fir woods has a thick coating of moss and almost no undergrowth, which means that even a large animal like a deer can move through them with hardly a sound.

He looked again, but the grey shape had gone, and he walked on thinking no more about it. A few moments later, however, he heard a laugh—a very hoarse, chuckling laugh, and this nearly startled him out of his wits, because he was sure there was no one in the wood but himself. He stopped then, and looked all around, but still there was not a soul to be seen.

"I'm imagining things," said he to himself, but he began

8

walking faster, all the same; and as he walked he thought that a fir wood was an eerie place to be in when all the tree-stems stood so tall and bare and dark against the strange half-light of a day's ending.

Hard on this thought he had another glimpse of the grey shape—ahead of him, this time; but this time also, although he saw it for no more than the blink of an eye, he knew it was not a deer. Then once again, he heard that same hoarse chuckle. A moment after that, and to his utter astonishment, a fallen branch lying on the path ahead of him seemed to rise in the air of its own accord. The branch moved back as if swung in the grip of some invisible person or thing, then it came rushing through the air towards him and hit him a mighty whack across the chest.

Colin almost went down under this blow; but it was also the very sort of thing to touch off his temper, so that now he was not so much afraid as angry.

"Stand still, whoever you are," roared he, getting his balance back, "and let *me* have a whack at *you*!"

The words were hardly out of his mouth before he threw his axe at the air above the place where the branch had been lying. He threw it hard, moreover, with an aim that was fast and true, and even although there was nothing at all to be seen ahead of him, the axe suddenly checked in mid-air as if it had hit something solid. There was a loud squeal of pain, the axe fell to the ground, and then—nothing! The forest was suddenly as still and quiet as before, and after a moment or so of listening to this silence and watching the stillness, Colin ventured forward to his axe.

Nothing happened to him when he bent to pick it up. There was no further strange thing to be seen or heard as he went on his homeward way; but now he had the ache of the blow he had suffered to make him cautious, and his eyes were every-where as he walked. His mind was busy too, trying to work out the meaning of it all, but by the time he had reached home he was still not a bit the wiser; and so he told himself that the best thing to do meantime was to keep a close mouth about the whole business.

After all, he reasoned, he could not swear to the fact that he had seen anything at all in the wood. And as for the story of something invisible hitting him with a branch and his own axe in turn hitting the invisible something—who would believe that? Even his own family, he decided, would say he had imagined it. And if they were foolish enough to cast the story abroad, it would only lead to other people laughing at him—which was something no man of pride should have to endure!

So Colin went to bed that night without having mentioned the least word of his experience in the wood, and feeling that this had been truly the wise thing to do. The next day, however, he was not so sure, because once again he thought he had caught a flashing glimpse of some odd shape flitting through the wood, and once again he heard the strange hoarse laugh that seemed to come from nowhere. That next day, also, everything went wrong for him.

Every time he felled a tree he found himself having to cut through the kind of knotted wood that blunted the edge of his axe. However neatly he judged the direction for a tree to topple to the ground, it always crashed over at some different angle. A pile of stacked logs tumbled down and almost crushed him. Then, on the following day, he had a further strange experience which altogether changed his mind about keeping his own counsel on the first one.

He had been working hard at the time, and was feeling a bit too warm. He took off his jacket, then he took off his bonnet, and laid them together on a tree-stump. Half-an-hour later he went to pick them up again, and found that his bonnet had vanished. He stood there for a minute feeling mightily puzzled about this, since there was no other forester within miles of him. Also, the bonnet had been a good one that was almost new, and the thought of losing it made him highly annoyed.

He looked all round the tree-stump, but still there was no sign of it. He cast in wider and ever wider circles, determined to find it but feeling foolish all the same about the search, since there was no wind that could have blown it so far away from where he had laid it. He did find it at last, however—much to his own surprise, because he had wandered far from the tree-stump by that time and had lost all hope of seeing his bonnet again. Yet there it was, lying beside a big, smooth boulder sticking from the mossy floor of the wood. And that was not the end of it, because part of this good new bonnet was almost worn through and there were threads from the worn part scattered all over the boulder.

Now it so happens that one sure way of working harm to a man is to get hold of his bonnet and rub it against something hard, saying curses all the while against that man. Then, once a hole had been worn in the stuff of the bonnet, the owner of it will die. Or so they say, at least, and the Grollican is such a spiteful creature that it takes great pleasure in trying to prove the truth of this saying.

Colin Grant was very well aware of all this; and so the moment he picked up his bonnet he knew what it was he had glimpsed and heard in the woods, and he also knew the reason for all the events of the past few days. He spoke aloud then, with horror in every tone of his voice.

"I'm being troubled by the Grollican!" said he, and set off immediately at the best pace he could, to tell his family this bad news and to let them know everything that had led up to it.

It was not so easy at first to convince his wife, Anna, she knowing very well that he was a man of some imagination; but once she had seen the worn patches on Colin's bonnet she knew that this was no made-up tale he had to tell.

"There isn't a doubt of it," she agreed then; and with her voice beginning to shake on the words, she added, "That is indeed the work of the Grollican."

"Then we must catch the wicked thing and teach it a lesson," declared Hector, the first of their twin sons.

"Yes, indeed we must," echoed the second twin, Hugh—because this was always the way of it with these two. They were not only as like one another in looks as two peas in a pod, they also thought alike and spoke alike, so that even their parents were sometimes uncertain which was which. Colin had no such problem at the moment, however, since he was equally impatient with them both.

"And tell me," he demanded of them, "just how do you expect to teach this lesson? The Grollican belongs to the Otherworld, remember, and it is always very careful to keep itself invisible. That means you'll never manage to take it by surprise. But even then, the most you could hope for would be the kind of glimpse I had of it in the dusk of the forest; and so how do you expect to catch it in the first place?"

The twins could find nothing to say to this, neither of them being much of a thinker; but it was quite the opposite case with their younger brother, Ian, and it was he who spoke up next.

"There's maybe some way of tempting the Grollican to show itself," he suggested; and would not be satisfied with the shake of the head that was all he got for answer.

"Why not?" he demanded. "What makes the Grollican so anxious not to be seen?"

Now this was not very easy for Colin to explain, because it meant telling first of all about one further creature of the Otherworld. This was the Voght, which is the mother of the Grollican, but which he had never seen although he had heard plenty about her. The chief thing he had heard, also, was that the Voght is a monster of ugliness—such a monster, in fact, that people cannot stand the sight of her.

"They do say, too," he added, once he had managed to explain all this, "that the Grollican is no better-looking than its mother. And if you ask me, that's good reason indeed for it to keep itself hidden from mortal eyes."

"Och the poor thing!" exclaimed Ian, thinking to himself how terrible it was for any creature to be so ugly that it was ashamed to be seen.

The rest of the family, however, were scornful of this tenderheartedness, which they thought was all very well for the animals Ian looked after, but quite out of place for a wicked one like the Grollican. It was only Anna, in fact, who did not entirely dismiss his sudden feeling of pity for the creature, and she quietened the others at last by remarking,

"And yet, you know, I have also heard tell that the Grollican is sometimes sorry for the things it does and tries to repair the damage."

"Much good *that* will do," said Colin, with anger getting the better of him again as he remembered the fright of finding his bonnet nearly worn into a hole.

"Well, then," Anna went on, "there's something else I've heard, for whatever it may be worth to you, Colin. The Grollican is large and hairy, and it has very big feet."

"How do you know that?" asked Colin, staring. "You're not going to tell me, are you, that *you've* seen it?"

"God forbid!" exclaimed Anna. "But this I will say, Colin.

I used to have a cousin who was troubled by the Grollican, and my cousin did once see the creature plain. Towards the end of his trouble, this was, at a certain moment when it was not on guard against being seen. So my cousin managed to take it quite by surprise, and from the one sight he had of it then, that was how he described it."

Colin felt dread beginning to creep over him. "And what happened in the end to your cousin?" he asked; but Anna just shook her head.

"Don't speak of it," said she, shivering. "He's dead now, God rest him. And maybe that wasn't the fault of the Grollican, but the poor fellow certainly never managed to get rid of it before he died. There's no man ever *can* get rid of the Grollican once it decides to trouble him—you know that, Colin. You know it every bit as well as I do."

The two of them stood looking at one another, and it was hard to tell then which of them was the more dismayed. Anna was a plump, handsome woman who had a fine rosy colour, as a rule; but now she had turned white as the moon. Colin's face was red and his thick dark hair was fairly bristling with temper, but for all that, he still had a scared look in his eye. He was not a man to be put down for long, however; and with all his family watching him, he knew he had to show a brave face.

"Well," said he at last, "there's one thing I'm decided on! I am not going to worry any further about the Grollican this night, because it cannot have any worse in store for me than the trouble it has already made. That's for sure! And so I'm going to settle down to my supper now—which is what we should all be doing by this time."

"That's right," agreed Hugh and Hector, much impressed by such a calm speech.

"Good for you!" cried Ian, seeing his father as a real hero now.

"Very sensible," agreed Anna, and put the supper on the table with the hope that matters might not turn out so badly after all.

So Colin managed to soothe the deepest of his family's fears, and to keep up his own courage that evening. But in his heart of hearts he knew very well that the Grollican *could* make even worse trouble for him; and he had not been many moments awake the next morning before he knew exactly what that trouble was.

2 Hunting the Grollican

It was the sound of his dogs barking which woke Colin that next morning.

There was nothing unusual about this in itself, of course, since all three of these dogs were kept chained outside the house at night, and early morning was the time when they would catch some scent that set them to making a noise—the sniff of a prowling fox, maybe, or rabbits venturing out to feed. At first, therefore, Colin paid them no attention at all; but the barking went on and on until it seemed to him that, this time, there must be something out of the ordinary upsetting the dogs. And so, most unwillingly, he got out of his warm bed to see what the something might be.

Outside it was a beautiful morning of bright sunshine with hardly a breath of wind moving, but Colin had not gone two steps beyond his door when it seemed to him that his croft had just been struck by a hurricane.

The wooden fence around his vegetable plot had been flung down and splintered to matchwood. The hen-coops in the yard had been smashed open and the hens scattered. The stable door had been torn from its hinges. The canvas covers had been ripped from the haystacks and the hay strewn wildly all over the place. Wherever he looked, in fact, there was such terrible ruin that amazement and despair held him quite dumbstruck; but it was not long before he found his voice again, and the yell he gave then brought all the rest of the family running to him.

Like himself, they could do nothing but stand staring in horror at all this. Then the first shock passed for them also, and Anna stammered,

"But—but how did it happen? There was no wind last night —there's none now, for that matter of it!"

"And it's not the work of anyone in this glen!" exclaimed Hugh. "We have no enemies here."

"Not one," agreed Hector. "And so who *could* have done it?"

"The Grollican, of course," shouted Colin, almost beside himself with rage by this time. "Can you not see that? It's the Grollican bringing trouble on me again!"

"What makes you so sure of that?" asked Hector; and Hugh protested,

"You've no proof it was the Grollican."

"There's proof in plenty before your very eyes," Colin said furiously. "What creature except the Grollican has the strength to lay the place in ruins like this? And who else would be spiteful enough to do so?"

"You have a point there," the twins admitted.

"Besides which," said Ian, who had immediately begun to free some chickens trapped in a wrecked hen-coop, "I have found a different kind of proof!"

He pointed to the dry, dusty ground beside the hen-coop, and all the others crowded towards him. They bent to look where Ian was pointing; and there, plain to see in the dust, were the footprints of some large creature. It might have been a human creature too, from the shape of the prints, but it was still no human which had made them. They were much too big for that. Furthermore, they showed only three toes to each foot; and where there should have been the shape of a heel, there was instead, the shape of a hoof.

The twins exclaimed in excitement at the sight of these prints, but Anna looked ready to faint with fear, and even Colin himself could not help feeling a touch of alarm. His scalp tingled, the hairs on his neck rose, but that did not stop him bending to look closely at the footprints.

"Well, that settles the matter," said he, straightening up again, and immediately went over to where the dogs were chained.

"No, Colin!" shouted Anna, guessing what he meant to do, but Colin was too set in his purpose by this time to heed her shout.

"You two get this place cleared up," he told the twins. "And as for me, I'm going to hunt the Grollican!"

On this word, he released the dogs; and, in high excitement, all three of these began jumping up at him. Colin soon had them in order, however, and when they were all still again and quietly waiting his next command, he turned at last to answer Anna.

"I know you're worried," said he. "But just think, Anna. The dogs don't have to be able to see the Grollican to track it. The scent from these footprints is all they need, and a chance like that may never come my way again."

"I don't have to think to know what will happen now," Anna said tearfully. "I can feel in my bones there's disaster ahead for you, Colin; and I'm telling you that the Grollican is much too cunning to be hunted by you or anyone else."

"Maybe so," Colin admitted. "But the chance is still too good to miss. And if there are any dogs at all that can be a match for it, it will be these three."

Without any more argument then, he led the dogs towards the strange footprints. They sniffed eagerly, drawing the scent from the footprints deep into their nostrils.

"On!" Colin commanded them, "On you go!" and the dogs bounded forward, with himself following at their heels.

"I'm married to a fool," said Anna, watching him out of sight. But Ian and the twins realised that this was only her worry for Colin speaking, and there was both envy and admiration in the glances they sent after him. As for Colin himself, there was nothing now that could have made him yield such a chance of hunting the Grollican, and all his hope of success in this was pinned to the fact that each of his dogs happened to have a special quality suited to that purpose. Indeed, it was for its special quality he had named each one of them, and the order of the chase now showed how well he had chosen these names.

It was Fios, the smallest of the dogs, which led the way, because it knew all that could ever be learned about tracking, besides a great deal more than any other dog had ever discovered. And this was just as it should be, since Fios is a word from the Gaelic language which was spoken in the Highlands in those days, and the meaning of it is "knowledge".

Running behind Fios came the tall, lean dog called Luath, which is the Gaelic word for "swift"; and this again, was the way it should be, because Luath could run fast enough to leave one wind and catch another. But the time of Luath would not come until a swift dog was needed to overtake the Grollican's last flight for freedom; and that was why the runner, Luath, still followed behind little Fios, the wise tracker.

Still further behind Fios and Luath came the very big and heavy dog with the Gaelic name of Trom, which means "weighty"; but Trom was not only a heavy dog. It was so strong, too, that it could pull down a running stag in full flight; which meant that this order would also be the final order of the hunt, because—once Fios had tracked the Grollican and Luath had overtaken it—only the great weight and strength of Trom would be able to drag it to the ground.

And then, Colin told himself, he would be able to wring a firm promise from it never to trouble him again; and so, at last, he would be rid of it! With this cheerful thought in his mind he kept urging the dogs on, but still their pace was not very fast because the Grollican had twisted and turned in its path, almost as if it had known Colin would track it from his croft.

There was still no deceiving Fios, however, not even where the Grollican had played the tricks a hunted deer will play to throw dogs off its scent—leaping from side to side of a stream, for instance, so that the dogs are left running aimlessly up one bank and down another. Sometimes, also, a deer will go back on its own trail, then take a leap that lands it many yards away on an entirely new track, with the old one seeming to finish suddenly in nothing. Either that, or it will paddle up and down in running water before it takes its leap away on another track.

All these things, it seemed, the Grollican had also done. Yet still little Fios kept its scent, and still it led the others steadily forward; until suddenly, tall lean Luath pricked up its ears and sniffed the wind. Fios also raised its head from the trail at that moment. Trom growled, sniffing the wind as Luath had done; and from all these signs, Colin knew that the dogs had at last sensed themselves to be within striking distance of the Grollican.

Now, he thought—now was the time to let Luath run the creature to ground. There was open moorland ahead, and he would be able to keep sight of the chase for quite a distance yet! A shout and a slap to the flank told Luath his wish, and like a steel spring released, the swift dog leaped into action.

In great, effortless bounds it flew ahead of them over the moor, moving faster than the wind that blew there, floating lighter than the thistledown carried by the wind. Colin raced after the long, flying form, wildly yelling his excitement in the chase. Fios scurried in front of him, barking as wildly as he yelled. Trom lumbered gallantly along at Colin's side, its great mouth open on a deep-throated roar.

There was still nothing at all to be seen ahead of them, of course; but Luath was following such a straight line over the moor that Colin knew the scent must be strong enough to make it certain the Grollican was lurking invisibly there. Perhaps in the shadow of the fir wood at the further side of the moor, he thought; and Luath had indeed almost reached the first line of trees in this wood before its forward flight suddenly checked.

Snarling, it whirled around and crouched low, with its back to the trees. A second later it was up again to start patrolling swiftly back and forward along the edge of the moor. Colin's guess from all this was that Luath had overtaken the Grollican, and was now trying to bar its way into the wood—which was so exactly according to plan, of course, that already he felt victory within his grasp.

"Good boy, Luath!" he yelled. "Hold it there! Hold it till we reach you!"

A roaring sound answered this yell, a loud and angry roar like the bellow of an enraged bull. The sound came from the part of the moor that was cut off from the trees by Luath's patrolling movement, and it struck Colin that this must be the Grollican roaring its anger at being caught in such a situation, but he was too excited by this time to let such a thought frighten him.

The scurrying form of Fios made straight for the sound. Trom pulled ahead of Colin, breaking into a lumbering gallop as it strove to catch up on Fios. Moments later, all three dogs were in action against the Grollican—still roaring its anger, yet still, in spite of that, refusing to let itself be seen; but even although this meant the dogs had to continue working by scent alone, they all acted with such purpose then that Colin felt like a blind person by comparison.

Luath began weaving a circle that would hold the Grollican pinned to the one spot. Fios darted in and out of this circle, nipping with its sharp teeth at every forward dart. Trom leaned back on its haunches, snarling, then threw all its mighty weight forward and up in the kind of leap it would have made to carry itself to a grip on the throat of a stag.

The leap was checked in mid-air as sharply as if Trom had clashed into a brick wall, but the big dog's jaws had closed on something at the height of that leap, and it hurtled to earth sprawling astride of this something.

"Good dog!" yelled Colin, panting forward in triumph to this scene. "You've got the Grollican!"

Fios and Luath closed in at the same moment, and instantly the ground was a snarling, snapping mass of dogs with the most terrible heaving and roaring going on in their midst. Colin shouted again, his triumph turning suddenly to dismay, because it had never been in his mind that the dogs should really hurt the Grollican; but now it seemed they were in a fair way to doing so.

A very large and three-toed foot came thrusting out from the mass of snapping, twisting, snarling dogs. Then, to Colin's even greater dismay, the heaving movement underneath all that wild fighting began to dimly take the shape of something large, and grey, and furry. It was the Grollican, becoming visible against its will, he realised. And that could not be happening unless the creature had indeed been wounded—so badly wounded it could no longer call up the power that kept it from being seen.

"Leave it!" Colin yelled, and plunged forward at the same time, meaning to wrench the dogs off the creature. "Fios! Luath! Trom! *Leave*, I tell you!"

That was the last thing Colin knew for a few moments, because he never did manage to grab hold of his dogs. Instead, he found himself stumbling from a mighty blow to the back of the head; and when he came slowly to the world of sense again, he was lying where the blow had tossed him, many yards away from the fight.

The fight itself, moreover, had taken on a very different appearance, because—although they were still on the attack —the dogs no longer had the mastery of it. Also, it was no longer the Grollican which was the centre of their attack. Instead, it was some huge kind of monster that was all too plain to the view and so horrible to look at that even a single glance made Colin feel quite faint again.

Its face, he saw, was green, like old green leather. The eyes that glared from this face were huge, and red as glowing coals. Springing from the head and growing all down the neck, there was a long green mane of horse-hair. Instead of hands and feet, the monster had hooves, and there was a long tail of green horse-hair sweeping the ground behind it. Yet still, in spite of all these things, the creature was not a horse. Neither was it human, even although it reared upright on two legs. And yet, Colin shuddered to see, it was a woman's clothing that covered its huge and shapeless body!

Colin was still in a bit of a daze, mind you. Otherwise, he would have realised straight away that this monster was none other than the Voght, the mother of the Grollican, coming to the aid of her son—as she always does, of course, whenever that creature over-reaches itself and runs into danger as a result. One thing, however, Colin certainly did realise, and that was the fierce course of the battle going on between the monster and his three dogs!

Each of these, as usual, was playing the part best suited to its size and build, with little Fios darting in to nip at the monster's hind limbs, Trom charging heavily to try for a grip on its throat, and Luath's great speed carrying it back and forward in one slashing leap after another. As usual, too, all three were fighting like a team, each one watching the others and timing its attacks to take advantage of their moves; yet still the monster was managing to hold all three of them at bay.

The kick of a hind hoof sent Fios in a backward spin across the grass. The downward stroke of a forehoof caught Luath in mid-leap. A tremendous butt of the monster's head countered the charge of Trom. The dogs snarled, shook themselves, and came in again. And again the monster beat them off, lashing out with its hooves, butting with its hideous green head, its great body whirling to cover every angle of attack.

The dogs tried confusing it with half-moves and false rushes. The monster snorted with anger, but held steady and would not be drawn. The dogs mounted yet another attack—and another, and another! The monster was still a match for them, butting, slashing, and kicking in all directions, and Colin was about to tell himself that he had never seen anything like this before in his life, when he suddenly realised it would not be true to say that.

There had been another occasion, he remembered, and the creature that held his dogs at bay then had been a cow from his own herd. What was more, that cow had turned on them with the same fierce, blind courage the monster was showing now, kicking and butting till she had all three of them not only pinned down, but in danger of being badly hurt as well. And the cause of it all was simply that the dogs had been helping him to take her calf away from her. That was why the cow had fought so fiercely—to guard her calf!

It was on the instant of this memory wakening in him that Colin realised this monster was the Voght, and he knew also how he himself had come to be struck down. The Voght had heard the roaring of its son, the Grollican, and had come rushing to its aid. He himself had been in the path of its first blow. And now, while the son made good its escape, the monster mother was fighting savagely to hold off his dogs— so savagely indeed, that she was bound to do more than injure them!

As if to ram this thought home to Colin, the Voght lashed out with a kick that caught Fios in the flank and sent it hurtling through the air to crash down beside him. Colin staggered to his feet, groaning as this wakened the pain of the blow he had suffered, and with all the strength he had left to him, he called the other two dogs.

They hesitated, turning their heads towards him, then snarling as they faced around to the Voght and made to begin another attack. But they were beaten by this time and both of them knew it. The attack was a half-hearted one, and when Colin called again they began slinking back to him—yet this, of course, only gave him a new problem.

What would he do, he wondered, if the Voght pursued them and then attacked *him*? Little Fios had not moved from where it lay, which meant that some of its ribs might have been broken by the final kick it had been dealt. Luath and Trom had given up the fight. He had no weapon he could use to defend himself against the monster, and he would never be able to run fast enough to escape from it!

Anxiously Colin watched Luath and Trom with one eye and the Voght with the other while he told himself what a fool he had been not to have brought his forester's axe with him. Yet still he could not help hoping that the Voght would be content with the escape of its son, the Grollican, and the victory over the dogs—and so, in the end, it proved to be. The Voght stood for a few moments sending the glare of its great red eyes after Luath and Trom. Then, with a loud snort and a shake of its long green mane, it made off triumphantly into the trees at the edge of the moor.

Colin felt his knees go weak with relief at this, but it was only when it had vanished entirely among the trees that he felt safe again. The dogs were his first thought then, and when he bent to examine them he found that Luath had a torn ear and a great gash along one shoulder. Trom was limping badly on one hind leg, and his muzzle was bleeding. As for Fios, there was no doubt at all about those broken ribs, and the only question was how to save it further pain.

As gently as he could, Colin lifted the little creature and prepared to carry it home. Then he looked from one to the other of all three dogs—the wise little one, the lean swift one, the strong heavy one. Together, he thought, they made the most perfect team that any man had ever owned. Together, they were the only dogs which could have succeeded in hunting the Grollican. Yet even they had failed in that; and to see them all bleeding and injured as they were now, just about broke his heart.

"It was my fault entirely," said he, speaking aloud as if they could understand him. "But I would never have set you to hunt the Grollican if I had thought *this* would happen. Believe me,

I wouldn't! And believe me also, I'll never ask such a thing of you again."

With remorse nearly choking him then, he started off for home with Fios in his arms and the other two limping behind him; but even a small dog can be a burden when it has to be carried carefully for miles, and Colin was in no great shape for such a task. As for Luath and Trom, they were not only suffering from their wounds, they were also exhausted by their fight against the Voght; and so it was a very sorry procession which finally arrived home that day.

Anna cried out in dismay at the state they were in, but she also rushed to fetch ointment and bandages; and while she and the boys doctored all the wounds, Colin told them of the Voght and the great fight it had put up to let the Grollican escape.

"And so there you have it," he finished the story. "All I have managed to do is to prove I cannot hunt the Grollican, no matter how badly it chooses to trouble me. I can do nothing to harm it, in fact, or the Voght will appear again to protect it from me. And goodness knows there isn't a man alive would risk a second time of facing *that* monster!"

Anna threw up her hands in despair. "Then it's just the way I said," she exclaimed. "You'll never get rid of the Grollican— never!"

"Not until the day I die, it seems," Colin agreed gloomily, and the two of them looked at one another, each reading the same question in the other's fearful glance.

What trouble did the Grollican have next in store?

3 *The Strange Woman*

"GET THE place cleared up," Colin had told Hugh and Hector, and they were good, willing lads. They did their best to obey him, but their best could still not mend all the damage the Grollican had done, and Colin was too shaken by his encounter with the Voght to tackle anything else that day.

"But tomorrow will be time enough," Anna told him. "The work will not run away in the meantime."

"Is that meant for comfort?" demanded Colin with a flash of his old temper. "Because, if it is, I can do with comfort of a different kind."

When Colin went out of the house the next morning, however, he found a surprise waiting for him. The stable door had been hung back on its hinges. The fences had been mended, the broken slats of the hen-coops nailed up again, the yard swept clear of wreckage. All the work the twins had started to do, in fact, was now completed. It had all been done rather clumsily, mind you, but it had still been done, and the moment Colin grasped this situation he knew what it meant.

"Come and see this!" he shouted to the rest of the family, and when they all came running out he told them,

"Look! The Grollican has been back. And it has tried to repair the damage it did."

With eyes of wonder the others looked all around, and Anna exclaimed,

"Well, would you credit that! But it shows you, doesn't it? Everything I've heard about the creature *must* be true."

"I'll tell you what else it shows," said Colin. "The Grollican discovered yesterday it had gone too far with me, and it was the fright the dogs gave it that told it so. Which means that the twins were right, after all, to say we should teach it a lesson, even although none of us could see at the time how that might be managed. What's more, it's my guess that this is not the first time the Grollican has had such an experience, and that's why they say it sometimes tried to mend the damage it does. *That's* why it's sometimes sorry for its wickedness."

Hector nodded wisely to this argument, and so did Hugh—as well they might, of course, seeing it had made the pair of them sound so sensible. Ian took a different view of it, however; his tender heart having being touched by the efforts of the Grollican.

"You're being a bit hard, are you not?" he asked. "Maybe the Grollican doesn't really want to be so wicked as it seems to be, and if that's so, it will have a conscience about the things it does. Maybe that's why it sometimes tried to set them right."

"Conscience!" Colin echoed scornfully. "It's you that has the great imagination, boy. You'll be having us all weeping for the poor Grollican if you go on like that about it!"

This raised a laugh from the others, but although Ian blushed to hear them laugh, he still felt in his heart that he might have got nearer the truth about the Grollican than his father had. Colin himself, however, was absolutely sure that *he* had the truth of the matter, and so now he felt a great deal more cheerful about everything.

"You'll see," he promised the others. "Whatever the Grollican does to trouble me in future, it will still be careful not to go too far again. You mark my words on that!"

The others all nodded, although Ian continued to think his own thoughts; but as the days passed by after that, it began to seem that Colin had been right after all. There was more trouble from the Grollican, certainly, but only in a small way. It stole tools from Colin's shed, for instance, and left them out in the rain to get rusty. When he was in the forest, it set branches across the path to trip his steps, and lurked invisibly about to laugh at him when it succeeded in this. Sometimes also, it blunted his axe, or hid the ropes he used for hauling timber, and laughed again when Colin's quick temper made him rage and shout over all these things.

It was cautious of its own safety too, in playing such tricks on him, because all three of his dogs were now recovering nicely from their first encounter with it. It kept well clear of them, therefore, never allowing them to scent it again—which did indeed seem to prove that they and Colin had taught it a sharp lesson. That was some satisfaction to him, at least. Besides which, of course, he was relieved that the dogs were having the peace they needed for their wounds to heal properly.

There was still one other thing, however, which annoyed Colin at this time. The Grollican never troubled any other member of the family; and so, even although he was sure he had now forced it to keep its antics within bounds, he began to resent being singled out in this way.

It was unfair, he thought, that the Grollican should amuse itself by teasing him just because he was the quick-tempered one of the family. He had not asked to be given a temper, after all. He had been born with this fault in his character, and who could blame him for that? What was more, he was always sorry afterwards if his temper had hurt anyone's feelings, and every-body knew that was so.

So Colin argued to himself, never once thinking that it was all very well to be sorry for any harm his temper had caused, but that the proper thing to do was to try mastering it in the first place. The result, of course, was that all his arguments went round and around in his head without ever coming to any con-clusion, and he got into such a fret over this in the end that there was no living with him.

"Away and take a walk to yourself," Anna told him one evening. "Go up the hill. Talk to the cattle you have up there, because you are certainly no company for any of us, the way you are now."

"I'm no company for anyone at all, the mood that's on me," Colin agreed; and thinking that the walk might at least serve to calm his mind, he decided he would go up the hill behind his house and take a look at some cattle he had put out to pasture there.

Away he went towards the grazing-ground on the upper slopes of the hill, but as soon as he drew level with this grazing-ground he realised that even there he was not alone. On the far side of the pasture he could see a woman, a young and slender woman dressed in green with a golden chain around her waist, and this woman was coming towards him.

The woman drew nearer and he saw that she was not only young, but beautiful, with a face like a flower in its first bloom and long hair as bright and golden as the sun. Moreover, the stuff of her green gown was silk; she wore a bracelet and collar of gold as well as the golden chain around her waist. And who but a lady—a rich lady at that—would dress in silk and gold to take an evening stroll on the hillside?

Colin was most impressed, but the lady was not at all haughty or proud with him. Pleasantly she gave him the time of day, and since he was a man with an eye for a good-looking woman, they were soon talking in the friendliest way. Even so, the lady still gave no hint of who she was or where she lived, which made Colin very curious about her. The more they talked, the more this curiosity grew, yet the more they talked the less opportunity there seemed to be for putting the kind of questions in his mind; and so, at last, Colin gave up all thought of asking these.

He was content, instead, to look and listen, and to think that never before had he heard anything like the music of the young woman's voice, or seen any face so beautiful as hers. Then, out of all this fascination, there came a moment when her red lips tempted him to a kiss, and to his delight, the young woman seemed quite agreeable to this.

Her arms came warm and soft around his neck. Her lips met his—and never had he felt a kiss so sweet! On the instant, he was drowning in love for her. On the instant also, however, he had the answer to all his wonderings about her and knew himself to be a lost man, for the very sweetness of that kiss told him it was no mortal creature he held in his arms!

This was a woman of the fairy people. And he should have guessed that before, from the gown of green silk and the golden hair—for was not this always how the old stories told the appearance of a fairy woman? And did not these stories also say that one kiss from a fairy woman was enough, not only to make a man fall instantly in love with her, but also to put that man completely in her power?

Colin felt his senses beginning to go from him. It was too much to happen to any one man, he told himself; first the trouble with the Grollican, and now the fairy woman— who was doubtless planning, there and then, to carry him off with her and make him live forever in thrall to her and her kind.

With bitter regrets he drew back from the kiss, thinking how strange a love was this, and how much more kind and tender was the love he had for his own dear wife, Anna. Besides which, he wondered mournfully, what would become of Anna and their three boys when the fairy woman carried him away to *her* people?

"You're not yourself, are you?" asked she, staring at the long face Colin now wore.

"I'm not the man I was a few minutes ago, and that's the truth," he confessed. "But can you blame me for that—you that has me in your power now, to do with as you will?"

"So you've guessed who I am," said the fairy woman, smiling; and dolefully, Colin nodded.

"Aye," said he. "And more fool I was to kiss you; for if there is one thing I do not want it is to live in thrall to you and your kind, the way they say these things happen."

The fairy woman laughed at this, but her laughter was not cruel. "There's no need to believe all you hear," she told him cheerfully. "And there's no need to go with me if you would rather stay with your own kind. *I* am quite content with stolen kisses, and so you are in no danger from me."

"Well," said Colin, feeling most relieved at this, "that's generous of you, I'm sure. But I'm a married man, you know, and that's something I should have remembered before this. I'll not be seeing you again, I fear."

"But you will!" exclaimed the fairy woman. Then, as Colin made a hasty bow and prepared to leave, she repeated mockingly,

"You will!"

"*You will ... you will ... you will ...!*" All the way down

33

the hillside Colin seemed to hear the following echo of that mocking cry. All the next day he thought of it, and of the beauty of the fairy woman. There was no further trouble from the Grollican, either, to distract him from these thoughts, and by the time evening came he could not resist slipping away to meet the fairy woman again.

She was waiting for him at the grazing-ground, as beautiful as he remembered her. Like a man under a spell—which indeed he was—he went towards her. And like some magic creature made of gold and flowers and sunshine and music—which indeed she might have been—she drifted into his arms.

Once Colin had parted from her, of course, his conscience smote him again, and he thought how terrible it was that he had so deceived his own dear wife as to meet secretly with another woman—even although that woman was no mortal creature. Yet still he was so lost in love for the fairy woman that he could not resist going back the next evening to meet her yet again. And it was then that he learned he had the Grollican to blame for this situation also.

"What a lucky chance for me you came walking by on that first night we met," said he fondly that evening to his fairy love; and at this, she laughed.

"It's not chance you have to thank for that," she told him. "It's the Grollican! *The forester they call Colin Grant is a fine, handsome man*, it said to me. And it also said, *He has an eye for good-looking women, too, and he pastures his cattle on the hill behind his house.* Then it talked some more till it had me persuaded to come along and see this handsome forester for myself. And *that* was how we met!"

Now Colin had been so sure he had taught the Grollican a lesson that all this threw him into a terrible confusion. He gaped, first of all, hardly able to believe his ears. Then he roared with anger to think of himself all unsuspecting while the Grollican planned to bring him under the spell of the fairy woman; after which, his one thought was to go straight home and confess his whole fault to Anna. By this time, however, the fairy woman had fallen as much in love with him as he was with her, and she coaxed him so sweetly to stay a while longer with her instead that Colin could not help but agree.

"What shall I do?" he asked himself when he had finally left her that evening. "What *shall* I do?"

It was dreadful to think he would never have met her at all if it had not been for the Grollican's trickery; but now that he had met and fallen in love with her, it seemed even more dreadful to have to part from her. On the other hand, what could be worse than to go on deceiving poor Anna?

So Colin wrestled once more with his conscience—the difference this time being that he also had to consider it was the Grollican that had caused his situation in the first place. And why should he allow the Grollican's spite to triumph over him? Colin could not endure this thought; and so, on the following evening, he made up his mind to resist the idea of meeting the fairy woman ever again. He was a man under a spell, however, which meant that he had little control of his actions, whatever his mind might say.

Hard as he tried not to think of the fairy woman, it seemed to him that he could still hear her calling, calling to him. Much as he tried to ignore this call, he still heard it like a voice inside his head, and the sweet temptation of it was too much for him at last. Up the hill he went, to the side of his love, and when he told her of the way he had seemed to hear her voice inside his head, she had laughter waiting for him.

"Now you know the measure of the hold I have over you," she told him. "Nor will you break that hold unless you can resist my call for one whole night, for it is only with the coming of white day that my power vanishes. But no man ever has succeeded in resisting the call for a whole night, and so that will never happen."

"Then pity me and let me go of your own free will," Colin begged, but the fairy woman would not have this. With more laughter and kisses, she stopped Colin's mouth until he was as foolish in love as before; and in this way, another week went by. Every evening Colin tried to resist temptation, but every evening the fairy woman's voice sounded inside his head, calling him to her. He could not help himself answering her call, even although he knew the Grollican must be laughing to see this happen. And when Anna began wondering aloud why he had taken to going up the hill every evening, instead of just occasionally, he made an excuse out of the cattle he had up there.

"Those beasts don't seem to be flourishing as well as they should," he told her, "and I'm just keeping a constant eye on them till things improve."

At the end of that week, however, Colin began to notice that there really was something wrong with his cattle. They lacked the shine that healthy beasts should have to their hides. They were thin, in spite of the good grass on that part of the hill; and before his very eyes, the whole herd seemed to be dwindling and pining away.

"I cannot understand this," he told the fairy woman. "I just cannot. They were healthy beasts when I put them up here—and now look at them!"

"When you put these beasts up here," said she, "you were not being troubled by the Grollican."

Colin stared in sudden dread at this, wondering what was to come next.

"No more I was," he agreed. "But what has that to do with it?"

The fairy woman began to laugh, which Colin thought was heartless of her, considering the loss he would suffer if these unhealthy cattle died on him.

"It's got this to do with it," said she when she had finished laughing. "I know more about the Grollican than you do, and so I am telling you now that these are not the cattle you put to graze here. In fact, Colin, *they are not yours at all!*"

"Not mine?" echoed Colin, looking in amazement at her. "What do you mean by that?"

"I mean that the Grollican stole your cattle and put these in their place," the fairy woman explained. "And in case you doubt me on that score, let me also tell you that I saw it do so."

Colin flushed with anger at this. "Then where are mine?" he shouted. "What has that creature done with them? And who owns *these* miserable beasts?"

"Don't you shout at me!" the fairy woman told him sharply, "or I'll not tell you another thing about the Grollican."

"You do as you choose," roared Colin, "but these creatures are not staying on my land!" And quite beside himself with rage by this time, he sprang forward to drive the cattle off the hill.

"Be careful!" the fairy woman cried out, alarmed. "These are fairy beasts!"

Colin was too angry even to hear this warning. With yells and shouts, he dashed up to the cattle, seized the nearest one by the tail and gave it a great slap to make it run. The creature jumped forward, and all the rest of the herd surged after it. Colin ran with them, still shouting and slapping to urge on the beast he had by the tail. Its pace grew faster. The pace of the other cattle grew faster, and at last the herd was pounding along hard enough to satisfy him. He made to drop the tail he held, and stop running; but to his horror, found that his hand was stuck fast to it.

With all his strength Colin tried to pull free, yet still could not do so. The herd ran faster, faster, and faster yet. The beast he held kept pace with the others. And, willy-nilly, with great roars and bellows of alarm breaking from him at every step, Colin was dragged onwards with them.

4 A Gift of Magic

A STAMPEDING herd of cattle can run quite a distance before it calms down, but this one never did seem to calm down!

For mile after mile it thundered on, taking Colin with it over hill and moor, across streams, through woods, and crashing a mad trail among boulders and brambles. The poor man was bruised, whipped, beaten, pounded, and torn by all the obstacles in its path; yet still he could not let go the tail he gripped, and still he had to run as fast as the beast that owned the tail, or else he would simply have been dragged along full length behind it and so have suffered even more.

It was lucky for him, therefore, that he had always been a very active as well as a very strong man; otherwise he could never have kept his footing in such a chase. But Colin did not think of it in this way—so far as he was able to think at all, that is.

Every bruise and blow he suffered, every thorny branch of bramble that whipped across his legs, only made him more hot with anger against the Grollican; and what between this and wild desires for revenge on the creature, there was room for nothing else in his mind—not even the question of where the stampede was taking him. Gradually, also, he lost all sense of time, so that he had no idea of how far he had run when the cattle at last began heading for what looked like a large cave in the hillside ahead of them.

Like water pouring into a funnel they poured into the cave—which was not really a "cave" at all, Colin realised. It was a high, arched doorway with a huge single slab of stone for closing it swung to one side; and beyond this arch inside the heart of the hill itself, was a great hall.

The cattle stamped and snorted their way into this hall, carrying Colin with them; and, much to his surprise but to his relief also, the moment he was at its centre his hand came free of the tail he held. The cattle scattered from around him, and he was left standing there, quite dumb-struck with wonder at his new surroundings.

The hall, he realised then, was spacious and high-roofed. The light that filled it came streaming down from this high roof; and if stars could be lanterns, those were the lanterns he saw there. The roof itself was supported by great tall pillars that spread out branches at the point where they touched it; and if pillars could be trees it was trees which soared up to that roof and spread against it.

Colin got a crick in the neck from staring up towards all this, and so he looked down at the floor instead. But here was another wonder, for the floor of the great hall inside the hill was exactly like the surface of the ground outside it. Moss, grass, flowers—they were all there, and all seeming to grow as naturally in that starry, pillared place as they did outside in the open air.

Yet that was not at all natural, Colin told himself. Indeed, this whole place of stars and trees and flowers right inside the hill was so far from natural that it could never have been the work of human hands. Moreover, the fairy cattle had rushed into it like creatures thankfully reaching home, and so who except the fairy people themselves could have shaped it?

Fear gripped him at the thought, and suddenly he sensed that these same fairy people were all around him—invisible, yet still intently watching him. He turned to run; and, as if his movement had been the signal they waited, the creatures he had sensed made themselves instantly plain to his sight.

The emptiness of the hall was filled with their shapes. Its silence suddenly rang to their voices. The shapes surrounded him; and all of them were either men of the fairy people, or else they were women who looked like the woman of fairy he had met on the hill behind his own house.

Like her, the faces of these other fairy women were all bright and beautiful as flowers. Like her, they were dressed in green silk, with bracelets and brooches and collars of gold, and each one wore a girdle of gold around her slender waist. The men of the fairy people were as handsome as their women were beautiful. The flowing robes they wore were also of green silk; and they too, were richly ornamented with gold.

The green-clad figures closed in on Colin. Their bright faces smiled at him. Their voices struck shrill and chattering on his hearing.

"*He has brought our cattle back*", said some of the voices. And others said "*No, the cattle brought him!*"

The smiles grew into laughter, and one of the fairy people called,

"*Oh yes, the Grollican has a real spite at him, that's sure!*"

There was even louder laughter then, and Colin was so stung to fury by this that he forgot about his fear.

"Aye," he shouted. "And it was you that let him play this trick on me! It was *your* mangy cattle he took to put in place of my own good beasts, and I want those good ones given back to me!"

"That has already been done," one of the fairy women told him, laughing again. "As soon as you return to your own place you will find them there."

That took the wind out of Colin's sails all right, but he was fairly spoiling for a fight by this time, and so he came back swiftly enough to the attack.

"Then what's the point of it all?" he demanded. "Why did you let the Grollican have your cattle to exchange with mine in the first place?"

The fairy people looked at one another. "Why?" they echoed. Then one of them said,

"Because we like to laugh—that's why!"

"And now we've had a laugh at you," added another.

"The Grollican promised we would," said a third, "but we helped the laugh along ourselves with a spell that stuck your hand to the tail of the cattle-beast!"

This last remark was too much for the rest of the fairy people. They shrieked with laughter at it, pointing their fingers at Colin, and staggering about quite doubled up with mirth. He glared back in helpless rage at them, until suddenly he heard one hoarse, deep note of laughter sounding below their shrill voices.

He whirled towards this sound, just in time to catch a glimpse of the Grollican, or part of the Grollican, at least, because all he saw disappearing behind one of the great pillars was the back of a hairy head with shaggy pointed ears sticking from the top of it.

"Just you wait!" he roared at the fairy people then. "I know you have the Grollican hiding somewhere here among you, and I'll be revenged on it yet. But I'll be revenged on you too, for helping it—that's for certain sure. And *then* you'll laugh on the other side of your faces!"

Now if Colin had thought for a week he could not have said anything more likely to strike dismay into these same fairy people—the truth of the matter being quite simply that they had grown tired of the war between themselves and human kind. It had gone on for so many hundreds of years, after all—

this constant battle between their magical cunning and the power of Christian faith. Besides which, they were just beginning to realise there was no magic could defeat that faith; so that all they wanted, for a change, was to stay inside their own enchanted places and be at peace with the outside world of men.

The moment Colin vowed revenge on them, therefore, their laughter stopped. A terrible, waiting sort of stillness followed the sound of it. The fairy people turned to one another in this stillness, all the brightness gone from their faces. Then, in low sullen voices, they began to argue with one another.

"We could put a spell on this fellow that would hold him here for ever," said one. "And then he would not be able to do anything against us."

"But humans do not easily give up their own kind for lost," argued another. "And this one has a wife and sons."

"Aye, the wife and sons would search for him," chimed in a third. "Besides which, they know about the Grollican; and if they find one among their own kind who is wise enough to discover its trick with the cattle, they will soon trace this man to our hill."

"But they'll not dare come here without bringing a priest or a minister with them," cried another of the fairy people. "And you know what that means!"

"There will be Christian prayers said over us," muttered several of the fairies then; and the whole company flinched, as if they could already hear the blessed words.

"Or holy water sprinkled on us," cried others; and all the fairies wailed aloud at this, as if they had that very instant felt the dreaded touch of holy water on their skins.

Colin had not expected his threat to have such an effect, of course; but he was pleased about it, all the same, and his satisfaction was all the greater when one of the fairy people cried,

"Chase the Grollican out of here! We should never have listened to it in the first place!"

There was a great chorus of agreement from the rest. "Aye, it's all the Grollican's fault! Out with it—out!"

With one accord, then, all the fairy people turned towards the spot where Colin had glimpsed the hairy head and pointed ears. The loud and horrid sound of the Grollican roaring its anger came immediately from behind the pillar there; but still, in spite of that, the fairies began surging towards the pillar. Something flashed out from behind it, and with a noise like a hunting pack in full cry, the fairies gave chase to the something.

It was large and grey. That was all that Colin could have told about it before it vanished again from his mortal sight, but still he knew it could be none other than the Grollican. Moreover, he guessed, the Grollican would not be able to vanish from the sight of the fairies, since they themselves knew the secret of invisibility. And in this guess, of course, he was soon proved right.

With yells and shrieks the fairies rushed madly back and forth, pursuing the invisible figure of the Grollican the length and breadth of their hall. The noise they made mingled with the sound of its roaring, so that the whole place rang with the most shocking din, and Colin was thankful at last when the pattern of the chase showed they were driving it towards the hall's entrance way.

There they checked, and stood hurling insults after the Grollican, and warnings against ever trying to come back into their hall. Then, in twos and threes, they began coming back towards Colin—who had been taking delight in the rout of the Grollican, of course, in spite of being almost deafened by the noise it had caused.

"Well now," said he to the first few of the fairy people to

reach him, "you'll not lend yourselves to any more of the Grollican's tricks on me—will you, eh?"

"No," they told him ruefully. "We're not wanting anything nowadays but to live in peace with your kind. And we'll not do that if we let the Grollican bring *you* raging and threatening among us again."

"You will not," agreed Colin, feeling himself at quite an advantage now and deciding to make the most of that. "But there's still a bit more to this affair, you know, than chasing the Grollican from your hall."

The fairies were clustered all around by this time, and seeing how anxious these words had made them, he pressed home the advantage.

"What about the cuts and bruises I got when I was dragged on by that cattle beast?" he asked. "It was your spell that stuck my hand to its tail, and I'll need something from you if I'm to forgive you for that."

"Name it!" cried one of the fairies. "Tell us what you want."

"Name it!" others took up the cry, until they were all shouting together. "Name anything at all, and you shall have it from us."

Eagerly they looked at Colin, waiting to hear what demand he had. Boldly he returned their look, then let his eyes travel to the golden collars around their necks, the golden bracelets on their arms, the girdles of gold, and the gold brooches pinned to their silken clothes. There was no mistaking the desire in this look; and the moment they saw it, the fairy people began stripping themselves of the golden ornaments.

The bracelets, the collars, the brooches, the girdles, came showering at Colin, with eager hands continuing to toss them until he was standing ankle deep in a spreading heap of gold. And still the fairy people kept adding to this heap.

"*Take it! Take it! Take it!*" Shrilly their voices cried at him as they tossed more ornaments on to it. There was plenty more where that came from, they insisted, and if gold was what he wanted they were happy to buy peace with all they had.

Colin bent to fill his arms with this treasure, dazzled by the glitter of it, quite dazed by the thought of the fortune that was now his; but at the very moment his hands touched the gold, a voice whispered in his ear,

"You're a fool, Colin. It will all turn to horse-muck and dead leaves the moment you are out of here!"

With a start of surprise, then, Colin glanced in the direction of the whisper, and saw his own love among the fairy women standing close to him. She caught his look, put a finger to her lips to caution him against letting the others see she was acquainted with him, and whispered again,

"I've waited till this moment to let you see me, and now you must do as I say, or you'll regret it."

Colin nodded, pretending to be still quite taken up with the gold. The rest of the fairy people kept up their excited chattering, and under cover of all this his fairy love said quickly,

"Tell them you do not want any of the gold. And when they ask what you do want, this is what you must say.

> *Brown is the creature's hair and eyes,*
> *Gentle her nature, small her size.*
> *Day and night she can pull a plough,*
> *Yet never get tired. And I want her now!*"

Colin shot the fairy woman a glance of astonishment. "What kind of a creature is that?" he whispered back at her.

"One that lies under a magic," said she, "and one that they must give you if you ask for it in the words I have just told you.

But remember also, that you must never yoke it to anything except a plough, or that magic will be broken for ever."

Colin gave another nod at this, even although he did not understand why he should ask for such a gift, or why he should ask in such a way. Even so, it was his fairy love who had told him of the Grollican's trick with the cattle; and thus he had enough trust in her now to do exactly as he was bid. Furthermore, he argued to himself, he could well remember hearing it said that fairy gold did not last; and so, straightening up from the pile around his feet, and letting the few bits of gold he had gathered drop back among the rest, he called loudly,

"Wait—you have all made a great mistake about me! It's not your gold I want."

Silence, a sudden and watchful silence, came over the fairy people at this.

"But you looked at the gold," one of them said at last. "You looked at it with greed in your eyes."

"Of course," Colin agreed. "And who would not look greedily on such riches? But just think what would happen if I took so much as one of these golden ornaments home with me. I'm a poor man, and so people might think I must have stolen it— which would cost me the good name I am proud to have. On the other hand, there are some who might guess it was fairy gold—which would put you in fear of these same people coming here to look for gold for themselves. And so it would not be a happy thing for either of us, would it, if I took your gold?"

There was a further silence at this—an even more watchful silence than the first one, but finally, one of the fairy people asked,

"Then what *do* you want from us?"

Colin glanced towards his fairy love, but she avoided his eye. There would be no more help from her, he realised. She could

47

not run any further risk of letting her own people see she was his love. Nor would she dare let them suspect her of secretly telling him what gift he should demand of them.

"What *do* you want?" Others among the fairy people began repeating the question; and as the clamour of their voices grew ever louder, Colin took a deep breath to steady the sound of his own voice. Then, in exactly the words his fairy love had whispered, he answered,

> *Brown is the creature's hair and eyes,*
> *Gentle her nature, small her size.*
> *Day and night she can pull a plough,*
> *Yet never get tired. And I want her now!"*

There was a gasp from the fairy people; a great, indrawn gasp of amazement at these words, and then a ragged burst of protest.

"He's tricked us!"

"Some witch must have told him!"

"He can't have *that*!"

"Oh yes I can," Colin answered this last shout. "You told me you would give me anything I cared to name, and now I have named it. What is more, I have asked in the one way you cannot refuse, and you know that is so."

There was no getting away from the truth of this answer, of course, and the fairy people were well aware of that. They still had plenty of protests, all the same, and plenty of angry muttering among themselves before they finally agreed to let Colin have what he asked for. With a face of great annoyance on him then, one of the men went off into some distant part of the great hall, and came back from there leading a horse by its halter rope.

The horse was a young female—a filly as they call such a creature—brown-haired and brown-eyed as the rhyme had said.

True to the rhyme also, she was small—so small, in fact, that Colin almost choked with disappointment at the sight of her. That same rhyme, he told himself, had been nothing more than nonsense after all.

> *"Day and night she can pull a plough,*
> *Yet never get tired ..."*

How could that possibly be true of such a tiny creature? And why, oh why had he not taken the gold when the fairies offered it? There would have been at least a chance of riches in that, whereas this little brown filly looked too dainty and delicate to be of the slightest use for anything—let alone pulling a plough!

The bargain had been struck, however, and so he had to stick to his side of it, just as the fairies had stuck to theirs. Besides which, thought he with a look at the angry faces around him, they all seemed so upset over losing the little brown filly that there must surely be *something* remarkable about her! In a more cheerful frame of mind at this, he reached out to take her halter-rope. The fairy man who had led her in handed over the rope, and said, as Colin took this,

"There! You've got what you asked for, and you've already been told that your cattle are back where they belong. Does that satisfy you?"

"Not quite," Colin told him. "Not until I know you're telling the truth about my cattle."

The fairy man scowled at this. "Our word is our promise," said he. "And we *always* keep our promises."

Colin considered for a moment, and decided there was no sense in any further argument on that point. "Very well," said he. "It will still be a war between the Grollican and me. But once I have proved your promise to be a true one, it will be peace between me and your kind."

"Then go in peace," the man of the fairy people told him.

With a sullen look that belied these words, he stood aside to let Colin pass; and with sullen looks also, the rest of the fairy people made way for him to leave their hall. Colin went towards the doorway with the little brown filly walking behind him, quiet as a lamb at the end of her halter-rope. No one spoke, no hand was raised to stop them, yet still Colin felt the hair prickling on the back of his neck. At any moment now he thought, the fairies would change their minds about letting him go in peace; and it was all he could do then to stop himself breaking into a run.

Once outside the doorway and into the open air, he did start running. Nor did he slacken this pace until he judged he had put a safe distance between himself and the fairy people. The little brown filly followed meekly all this way, and when Colin stopped at last, he took another look at her—a much longer look than the first one he had given.

"*Gentle her nature . . .*" he thought then, and certainly she was easy to handle. There was a wise gleam to her eye, too, which pleased him; and altogether she seemed a likeable enough creature, in spite of her lack of size. He gave her a pat, on this thought, and smiled to find her pushing a nose as soft as velvet against his hand.

"So you're an affectionate beast, too, are you?" said he aloud; and then told himself that this was not really to the point. The important thing now was to discover if there was any truth at all in the last lines of the rhyme about this little brown filly. And there was only one test which could do that!

But first of all, he decided, he would have to make sure his cattle had indeed been returned to their own place; and it was with this thought foremost in his mind that he went on the rest of the way towards home.

50

5 *The Little Brown Filly*

COLIN NEED not have worried about his cattle, of course, since it is true enough that the fairy people always keep any promise they make. He would have done better, indeed, to have worried over how he was going to answer all the questions his family had to ask about how he had come by the little brown filly; but once he had made sure his cattle were safely back where they belonged, he brushed these questions aside and thought only of the test he had decided to make.

He was up early the next morning for that purpose, and away out to the stable where he had put the filly. He yoked it to a plough, and then called Hugh and Hector to him. Out they came, as ready and willing to work as always, only to stand amazed at what they saw.

"A creature so small will never be able to draw that plough," protested Hugh; and Colin told him,

"Maybe not, but that's what we three are going to find out. And if it *can* draw the plough, we'll take turns of working all day with it."

"You'll not work with it an hour, never mind a day," Hector insisted; but the argument was over so far as Colin was concerned, and he simply urged the little filly on to make the first furrow.

Off she started, stepping neat and light as a cat on her tiny hooves, yet pulling as strongly as any great cart-horse. Colin was astonished and delighted by this, and so were his sons; but even so, they all felt that the little filly must surely tire very quickly of such hard work.

Long before the day was out, however, they had all changed their tune. The little brown filly never faltered in her steady stride, never once slackened her efforts; and as the day wore on with each of them taking a spell of driving the plough, it was they who began to tire, instead. When evening approached, they gave her food and water. Then, turn and turn about, they went back to work again; and weary as they all were by that time, the little brown filly still seemed as fresh as ever.

Dusk fell, with Anna and young Ian coming out to find what was keeping them all so late at work; and the whole family was quite taken aback when Colin announced that they could go to bed if they wanted, but he was going to continue ploughing right throughout that night.

"But the three of you have worked that beast the whole day," Anna protested. "You'll kill it if you work it all night too!"

This was too much for Ian, who had taken a great liking to the little brown filly and was immediately much distressed to think of such a fate for her.

"Don't do that, Da," he begged Colin. "Don't kill the little filly."

Now Colin was fond of all his sons but, of the three of them, it was Ian who really had his heart. Also, since Ian's crooked shoulder meant he had never been able to play as heartily as children should, Colin was always willing to indulge him in other ways; and in this case, it was plain that any harm done to the little brown filly would greatly upset the boy.

On the other hand, Colin argued to himself, keeping the

creature all night at the plough was the only sure way of proving the claim made in the asking rhyme his fairy love had told him to say. Besides which, it was not every day that a man came into possession of a filly that might have magical powers, and he had to admit that his curiosity about these powers was growing stronger by the minute.

So Colin hesitated, glancing from Ian's anxious face to the little brown filly standing patiently between the shafts of the plough. She turned her head to look at him, and—just as he had done the night before—he noticed the wise gleam in her eye. *"The creature maybe has more sense than I have,"* he thought to himself, and it was this thought that solved his problem.

"I'll let the filly decide for herself," he told Ian. And immediately, the matter was settled.

The little brown filly started briskly off down the furrow, pulling strongly, treading neatly. Colin hurried to take a grip of the plough-handles; and so began the final test of all his fairy love had told him.

From hour to hour the little brown filly pulled the plough. From hour to hour Colin trod behind it. The rest of the family grew tired of watching and went off to bed. The moon rose, and shone steadily on the lone figures of man and beast. Furrow after furrow was tracked behind the plough, and the moon's pale light tipped their long dark lines with silver.

In the quiet of the night, the swish of the plough's blade through the earth came in soft, even waves of sound. The steps of the little filly beat a steady rhythm, and all this was sweet music to Colin's ears. The creature was indeed proving tireless, he thought exultantly; and there was money to be made out of that, because—quite apart from the ploughing she could do for himself—he would be able to hire her out to work on other

53

crofts! But in the quiet of the night also, Colin had thoughts which were of quite a different nature—long and solemn thoughts; and all of these, of course, concerned the Grollican.

Certainly, he told himself then, the business of the cattle had not turned out so badly for him. He had got his beasts back safely, after all, and now he also had this wonderful little filly. Besides which, he had been given the pleasure of seeing the Grollican chased from the fairies' hall, never to return. But what was he to do the next time it troubled him? What was he to do?

It was all very well flying into a rage and swearing he would get rid of the creature. The problem was how to keep such a vow, and losing his temper was not likely to help in that. Indeed, he realised glumly, this was something that never *had* done any good for him. It had relieved his feelings at the time, of course, but it had never made him any happier in the end. And certainly, it had never solved any problems for him.

So, without realising this was what had happened, Colin took the first great step towards solving this particular problem; because the moment a man faces up to a fault in himself, of course, is also the moment he begins to cure that fault. There was yet another problem in Colin's mind, however, and it was because of this that he did not see how far he had got with the answer to the first one.

When was he going to tell Anna about himself and the fairy woman? He would be a man caught forever in the trap of conscience if he did not tell her sometime. Yet it might well break her heart when he did tell her; so that, whichever way he turned, he was in trouble. And that, of course, was exactly what the Grollican had intended should happen to him!

Midnight passed, and Colin grew too weary to think any more. His legs began to ache from all the walking he had done, yet still the pace of the little brown filly did not falter. The white of dawn washed over the moon's silver light, and Colin almost fell asleep as he walked, yet still the little brown filly pulled strongly. Sunrise coloured the sky, and Colin's grip on the plough-handles became numb, yet still the little brown filly turned as neatly as ever at the end of each furrow.

Colin fell into a sort of dream where nothing seemed real to him any more, and it was only when he heard the voices of his family in the distance that he awoke from this dreamy state. He drew the little brown filly to a halt then, and took a good look at her. There was no sign of strain on her that he could see—no sweat on her coat, no drooping of her head. Her breathing was soft and even, her eye as bright as ever, and Colin knew then that he would no longer be able to avoid answering all the questions his family had asked about her.

To let them know the full truth, however, meant that he would also have to tell of his meetings with the fairy woman; and to speak of that in front of his sons would have put shame on him. He had a quick think to himself, therefore, and by the time they had all finished exclaiming and marvelling over the filly and her night's work, he was ready with a story that left out all mention of his fairy love.

He told it well, too, and it was near enough the truth to sound convincing. Besides which, the part the Grollican had played in it was enough to make them all hang on his words; but even so, the very first mention of the fairy people brought smiles from Hugh and Hector, and by the time Colin had finished speaking, they were ready to laugh outright.

"You're not expecting us to believe all that nonsense about fairies, are you?" asked Hugh.

"Because, if you are," chimed in Hector, "you'll be disappointed. We're a bit big now, after all, for fairy tales!"

Colin looked at his twin sons—so big, so grown-up, so sure they knew how many beans made five—and almost lost his temper with them. The lesson learned in the quiet of the night stayed with him, however; and so, instead of shouting at them, he said quietly,

"Just look at that filly, will you? She has ploughed by day and ploughed by night, never resting, never stopping; yet still she is not tired. Just look at the size of her. She's hardly any bigger than a dog. Look at the plough, and think of the strength it takes to pull it. And how do you think all that can be unless the filly has some fairy magic on her?"

Hector and Hugh looked as they were bid, then they glanced uneasily at one another, and Colin saw that they were not nearly so sure of themselves now.

"I'll tell you something else," he went on. "Now that the filly has proved the magic that makes her such a strong plough-horse, I plan to hire her out to other folk in the glen, for *their* ploughing. But there's one thing could put a stop to that. If the filly is yoked to anything other than a plough, all the magic will go from her. And I'll have the hide off you if you allow that to happen. Do you hear me? She must never, never be yoked to anything except a plough."

"We hear you," said the twins. "We'll be careful."

They spoke unwillingly, all the same, so that Colin could see they were still not convinced of the truth in his story. But young Ian was now eager to have his say and he had no such doubts.

"*I* believe the filly has a magic on her, Da!" he exclaimed. "And I'll look after her now, if you'll let me."

Colin looked at the gentle way he was petting and stroking the creature, and thought the two of them would get on very well together.

"Aye, I'll let you do that," he agreed. "But don't you spoil it too much or it won't be such an easy beast to work. And never, never forget you must not yoke it to anything except a plough."

"Trust me for that," promised Ian with his hands already busy at releasing the filly from the plough shafts.

As if to show her pleasure at this, she began gently nuzzling at his crooked shoulder, and soon he was leading her off to the stable. There he gave her good straw, and water. Also—as Colin had guessed he would—he stayed in the stable for a long time, talking most lovingly to her; and this gave Colin himself a chance to talk further to Hugh and Hector.

"Ask your mother about what I've said," he told them, "and see what *she* has to say about fairy people."

Now Anna Grant was nobody's fool. She had seen gaps in Colin's story that none of her sons had noticed, and so she knew very well that he had not told the whole truth about the little brown filly. But Anna also knew how to bide her time over such matters, and meanwhile, she realised it was important that the twins should not be allowed to deceive themselves over the fairy people.

"What I have to say," she told them, "is this. Many a one apart from your father has met with the fairy people; and many a one living in this glen could swear to the truth of that! Whatever *you* may think of them, therefore, I do not doubt for a moment that there are such creatures as fairy people. Furthermore, it is equally well known that these people have strange powers; and so I do not doubt for a moment, either, that they have put a magic on the filly."

The twins looked again at one another. They knew their mother for a sensible woman, not at all given to fancy; and so, when she spoke like this, they could not help but believe her.

None the less, they still had questions to ask, and Hugh put the first of these.

"What I do not understand," said he, "is why they have put *this* kind of magic on her. Why did they make her a plough horse? Why did they not do something better suited to such a little, dainty creature?"

"I can think of only one answer to that," said Colin. "The fairy people have always had cattle, but they have never had any crops because they have never known how to work the land. That means it would suit them fine to lay the filly under the kind of magic that would make it plough for them, day and night, without *them* putting out any effort."

"And why did you not say all this to begin with?" Hugh asked then. "Why did you keep us waiting a whole day and night before you told us anything about her?"

"It has taken long enough for you to believe me now," said Colin. "Would you have believed me then? Besides which, I was not sure, myself, of her powers until I had tested them."

This, at last, was enough to convince the twins; and once they had admitted as much, Colin told them,

"Away you go, then, and let me have a private word with your mother, for I have something to say to her that is not your business."

Away went the twins to have another look at the little brown filly, talking nineteen to the dozen about her as they went. Colin and Anna were left looking at one another, and even if he had not realised it already, Colin could have told then from the expression on Anna's face that the time for a full confession had arrived.

"Well now, Colin," said she. "It's time for the questions *I* have to ask. Who was it told you in the first place that it was fairy cattle the Grollican had exchanged with your own? And when the fairies told you to name the gift you wanted, *how did you know to ask for the little brown filly?*"

Colin bowed his head, thinking that the next few moments were not going to be easy ones. There could be no retreat from them, however; not now that Anna had shown up the gaps in the story he had told.

"I'm afraid there are other things you should know, apart from these," said he, and plunged straight away into his confession of everything that had happened between himself and the fairy woman.

"I'm heart-sorry for my fault, Anna," said he at the end of it all. "But you do see, do you not, that I would never have met the fairy woman in the first place if the Grollican had not put the idea of tempting me into her head. I would never have gone on meeting her either, if she had not put this spell on me that calls me to her side. And you do see too, I hope, that the Grollican's efforts to trouble me will be all the more successful if you do not forgive me now—for if you and I are at odds with one another, what else can there be in my life except trouble?"

Poor Anna just stood and stared at this, for she could see quite clearly that the trap the Grollican had laid for Colin in the first place had now caught her as well. If she forgave Colin, he would be free to go to his fairy love again; but if she did not forgive him, there could be nothing but anger and misery between herself and him. Yet there was one more question she felt she had to ask, and in a trembling voice, she did so then.

"Tell me, Colin," said she, "which of us do you truly love— me, or this woman of fairy?"

"Why, you, of course," exclaimed Colin. "It's not true love I feel for the fairy, Anna—it's only a spell of love she has cast on me. And if only I could resist it for one night, I would be free of her. I know that, for she told me so herself. Yet how can

I resist when I hear her voice calling, calling inside my head till I nearly go mad with longing to answer her call?"

Anna gave him a long, cool look. "I'll find an answer to that question," said she, "if you promise me one thing. The next time you hear her calling you, let *me* know about it. Do you promise that?"

"I promise," Colin told her, "although I don't see what good that can do."

"Neither do I at the moment," Anna answered grimly, "but I'll think up a plan soon—depend on it! There's no fairy woman going to have power over *my* husband. And only when I've made sure of that, Colin, will I forgive you."

This was Anna's last word on the subject, and Colin had to be content with it. But when he remembered the grim look on her face as she spoke he was not sure which was now the greater fear with him—the thought of being called again to the side of his fairy love, or the nature of the plan Anna might decide on to prevent that happening!

6 Breaking a Spell

FOR THE next three days after that there was peace of a sort for Colin and his family. The Grollican went back to troubling Colin only in small ways, and the fairy woman did not call him. On the other hand, there was scarcely a word passed between Anna and himself in all that time, which was not pleasant for either of them. Also, it seemed there were secrets between Anna and the twins, because the three of them were always whispering in corners, and this was something that worried Colin.

"You've not told them about the fairy woman, have you?" he asked Anna; and got a scornful look for his pains.

"Would I shame you in front of your sons?" she demanded then. "You should know me better than that, Colin Grant. It's the Grollican we're talking about. And if you want to know what I'm saying to the boys I am telling them of the way it works and warning them to be ready the next time it makes trouble for you."

"That's all right, then," said Colin. "But take care Ian doesn't hear you at it, because he's still young enough to be frightened by talk of the Grollican, and I'm not wanting that to happen."

"Ian is too busy with the little brown filly to hear his own name being called," said Anna; and she could not have spoken more truly, because Ian was now so enchanted with the filly that he gave his every waking moment to her. Indeed, he would also have slept beside her in the stable, if his mother had allowed it, and it was only after much argument that Anna succeeded in getting him back to the house each night.

So matters went on for yet another day, and Colin began to feel hopeful that the fairy woman would let him alone for good. The dangerous time of each day, however, was the evening, which was something that past experience had taught him only too well; and sure enough, on the evening of the fourth day he heard her calling him to the hill to meet her again. Immediately, then, he remembered his promise to Anna, and rushed to find her.

"I hear it, Anna," he gasped. "I hear that voice again, and I want to go to it, I want to go! Help me—please help me, Anna!"

"I'll do that," said Anna grimly, and pushing him down into a chair she ran to the door shouting urgently for Hugh and Hector.

The two boys came running to answer her, and to Colin's surprise, they brought a coil of heavy rope with them. Before he had time to ask the reason for this, however, Anna told them,

"The time has come, boys. Do what we agreed you should do. And if you love your father, do it well."

With one voice they answered her. "Trust us!" said they. Then, without another word spoken, they pounced on Colin and began tying him to his chair with the rope. This was entirely too much for Colin's dignity—a man like him to be tied up by two boys, and these boys his own sons!

"Let me go!" he roared. "Take your hands off me!"

"We will not!" panted Hugh, while both he and Hector pulled ever more strongly on the rope. "You'll not go out to meet the Grollican if we can help it!"

"We know there is a spell on you that makes you want to go," added Hector, "and then you would be in terrible danger. But the spell will be broken if only you resist it for one night. And that is why we *must* tie you down."

Colin was struggling so hard that it took a moment or two

before he understood what they were saying to him, but the meaning of their words pierced at last through the fog of anger in his mind. Immediately then, he stopped fighting to free himself, and sat quite still to stare at Anna.

So *that* was what she had been whispering to the boys, he thought. *That* was how she had avoided telling them about the fairy woman! She had warned them that he would hear a voice calling him out to the hill, and convinced them of the danger in answering that call. But she had also managed to convince them that the call would come from the Grollican. *That* had been her plan! And so here he was now, with both his sons still not knowing about the fairy woman, yet still tying him down so firmly that he would not be able to break free to meet her!

Colin's sudden stillness had given the twins the chance they needed to make really tight knots in the rope, and while all these thoughts were going through his mind, they got him trussed up as neat as a chicken ready for roasting. They stood back then, to let Anna have a look at their work, and while she bent to examine the knots, Colin could not help whispering to her,

"You're a clever woman, Anna."

"Maybe I'm not so clever as you think," Anna whispered back. "The twins are wondering why you've fallen so quiet."

Colin glanced at the twins and saw from their faces that this was indeed the case.

"Don't look so puzzled," he told them. "My temper is quick —I admit that. But it doesn't last, and I've sense enough to know when I'm beaten."

The twins lost their frowns then, and smiled instead. "That's good," said Hector, and Hugh chimed in, "There's no point in taking risks, after all—not where the Grollican is concerned, anyway."

"True enough," Colin agreed—a bit drily, it has to be admitted, for the fact that he admired the way Anna had managed things did not mean he was happy about spending the whole night tied to a chair.

A look at the faces of the other three, however, told him they had no intention of relenting over this—which was all to the good for Colin, of course, because the voice of his fairy love was still ringing in his head; and with every moment that passed, it seemed to him that he heard it more clearly.

The minutes stretched into an hour and the longing to run towards the sweet sound of that voice made him groan aloud. Anna and the boys talked to him, hoping that their voices would distract his attention from the one that tormented him. Yet still the silent music of it went on inside his head, calling to him on a note of such strange enchantment that no man could have described the beauty of it; and at last came the moment when he could no longer resist trying to answer that call. With a cry of despair bursting from him, he began struggling and straining to free himself of his bonds; but Anna was ready for that moment.

"Sing, boys!" she commanded the twins. "Sing a psalm against the power of the voice your father is hearing."

Obediently then, Hugh and Hector started up a psalm, as loud as if they were in church and the minister with his eye on them to see there was no shirking.

"*I to the hills will lift mine eyes*," they sang—this particular psalm being a favourite with the whole family—"*From whence doth come mine aid.*"

"Louder yet!" cried Anna; and, fairly roaring the words now, the two boys continued,

"*My safety cometh from the Lord, | Who heaven and earth hath made.*"

The strong young voices thundered on Colin's hearing, drowning out the sweet, plaintive cry of the fairy woman; and slumping back into his chair, he muttered thankfully,

"Good boys! Oh, good boys!"

And the twins really *were* good boys, his thoughts ran on. They were not clever, like Anna or young Ian; nor yet were they handsome, like himself. But no one could have asked for better sons at such a moment; and for that, he loved them! Anna met his eyes on this thought. She nodded to him, smiling; and under cover of the voices still bellowing away, she whispered,

"Hold out, Colin! The night will not last for ever."

"It will last for long enough," said Colin, gritting his teeth on the words. "And it would be against nature to expect the boys to sing until dawn."

"They promised me they would sing as long as their voices were needed," Anna assured him. And as Colin soon discovered, the twins had not lightly made this promise.

"*The Lord's my Shepherd*," they sang, the next time the sound of the fairy woman's voice tempted him to struggle against the rope. "*All people that on earth do dwell*," they sang the time after that. And all throughout that night, whenever there was need for it, they smothered the ancient power of her magic with the blessed words of another, and yet another psalm.

Colin began to feel less and less watchful, more and more sure he could last out the night—which was foolish of him, because a fairy that has a mortal in her power does not let him go all that easily. He was becoming very tired, too, which was something else that made him under-rate the cunning of the fairy woman.

His head nodded every now and then. He yawned, almost on the verge of sleep in his chair; and towards, dawn, there came a moment when his eyelids drooped, and closed. A sense of great peace stole over him; and gradually, it seemed to him, his whole mind was filled with a most beautiful vision of gold, and flowers, and sunshine.

Colin slept, and in his sleep the vision began magically shaping itself into the form of his fairy love. The golden glow of it became her long hair shining in the sun. The colours of it became the colours of her dress, her face, her lips, her eyes. The face smiled at him. The shimmering arms beckoned him into an embrace. Tenderly she spoke his name, and the sound brought him suddenly awake in such a rage of longing for her that all the psalms in the psalter could not have stopped him fighting free of his bonds.

Loud as the twins sang to him then, he still fought and strained against the rope; and, moment by moment, the coils of it began to loosen. Anna cried out in dismay at this, and quickly ordered the twins,

"Hang on to him, boys! Hold him down!"

Hector took one shoulder, Hugh grabbed the other, and together they pushed as hard as they could to make Colin sit still; but even that was no use. Big as they were, after all, they were still just boys, and Colin was a grown man in a frenzy that gave him more than his natural strength. Time and again he wrenched his shoulders free of their grip, and as the rope around him grew looser yet, Anna realised it was now the moment for some really desperate action.

Darting to the table, she picked up the long kitchen knife that lay there. With both hands clasped tight around the handle of this knife, she came back to Colin and stood in front of him.

"I'm warning you," said she, and held the knife so that the point of the blade was only a fraction of an inch from Colin's chest. "You'll break free of the rope at your peril, Colin, because *I* will not budge from this spot. And so, the moment you move to leave that chair will also be the moment this knife goes into your heart!"

Now it was Colin himself who was in the habit of keeping the kitchen knife sharp; and it was only the day before, that he had ground the blade. No one knew better than himself, therefore, how dangerous it was; and to see the long, keen point of it levelled against his heart like that, was enough to shock him into stillness.

"You couldn't!" said he in horror, looking from the knife to Anna. "Anna, you wouldn't!"

"Try me!" was all the answer Anna gave to this, but she spoke so fiercely that Colin hesitated to put her words to the test. With his eyes going back to the knife he remembered the way she had said, "There is no fairy woman going to have power over *my* husband!" And that was enough to make him realise there is *no one* more determined than a wife who is trying to keep her husband from another woman—even if that other woman is a fairy creature, and he under the spell of fairy love.

"A man is kind to his life," said he, sighing. "And that's a fact, Anna. You know I daren't try you!"

"Aye, and maybe you don't want to, now," returned Anna, thinking to herself that all this might have taken Colin's thoughts off his longing for the fairy woman.

"You're right," admitted Colin, for that was indeed the case. The shock of Anna's desperate action had quite driven the beautiful vision from his mind; and with pleasure and surprise as he realised this, Colin added,

"I want nothing more, in fact, than to stay here safely until morning!"

The knife began to shake in Anna's hand. "Praise be!" she said softly, turning the point away from him. "Oh, praise be!"

And from the twins, who had been as horror-struck by her desperate act as Colin himself, there came great sighs of relief. Colin sighed also, wondering if he would ever again be so near to death, and his face was so doleful then that Hugh said quickly,

"And you don't have long to go now, because it *is* nearly morning."

"That's right," encouraged Hector. "You've almost beaten the Grollican now, and if only you can hold out for another hour the spell of its call will be broken and the danger of this night will all be past."

Colin gave Anna a look which thanked her again for keeping the secret of the voice that called him. Then his eyes went to the clock and he saw that Hector was right. In less than an hour it would be morning—and what was more, the power of the fairy woman was becoming weaker with every minute that brought morning nearer! He could still hear her voice, it was true, but it was thin and faraway now as a small wind grieving over some distant land.

As for the beautiful vision, he thought, that could only have been her final, cunning attempt at working her magic on him. But Anna—his own, dear Anna—had defeated that attempt; and now that the fairy's power was fading, there would be no more visions to drive him mad with longing.

"You could tell the boys to loose me now," he suggested to Anna. "It would be safe enough, surely, now that morning is so near?"

"H'mm," said she. "It might be so, but—"

That was as far as Anna got before she was interrupted by a tremendous commotion of barking from the dogs chained outside the house; and right on top of the barking, came another noise that was like the bellowing of an angry bull. Anna started in alarm at all this, and turned a puzzled face towards the noise.

"In the name of fortune!" she exclaimed. "What on earth can *that* be?"

The twins followed her look, as startled as she was, and just as puzzled; but this was now the third time Colin had heard that angry bellowing, and so he guessed instantly what it was and what had set his dogs to barking. The Grollican was out there, roaring at the defeat of the fairy woman's spell, raging because it could no longer trouble him through that spell; and the thought of being tied at such a moment sent him into a terrible panic.

"Loose me, you two!" he shouted at the twins. "That's the Grollican you're hearing outside—d'ye understand? And so, quick now—untie the rope!"

With fear and dismay on their faces, Anna and the twins heard this shout, but the twins had their orders from Anna, and they were both determined their long night of effort was not going to be wasted.

"Never!" they shouted back at Colin. "If we untie you now, there will be no saving you from the Grollican!"

The roaring grew even louder, and through it came a crashing and a banging, as if the Grollican was trying to throw down the sheds and outhouses at the back of the house.

"Loose me!" Colin yelled again. "The creature is destroying the place!"

"Let it," the twins insisted. "So long as it doesn't destroy you."

"Anna!" Colin implored. "Cut the rope, please, and let me out to protect things from it."

"No," Anna told him. "You're safe here, and here you'll stay."

"But it could come into the house," cried Colin. "And then what would you do, with me trussed up here, and helpless?"

The words were hardly out of his mouth when there was a

terrific banging at the door, as if the Grollican were indeed trying to force a way in.

"I told you!" Colin shouted. "I told you that would happen!"

Hector seized hold of the poker. Hugh rushed to get his father's axe. Anna took a firm grip of the kitchen knife; but although she had grown white as snow at the banging noise, she still would not hear of letting Colin free. Stubbornly, for all that her voice trembled as she spoke, she told him,

"The Grollican *cannot* get into the house, Colin, because I have protected the doorway with a charm. And there is no creature of the Otherworld can pass over or through that charm."

Colin stopped struggling with the rope to stare at her, and the boys also stared.

"You did what?" they asked in astonishment; and Colin shouted, "For goodness sake, woman, *what kind of charm?*"

Anna bit her lip, because the charm she had used was to kill a calf and sprinkle the doorposts with some of its blood. Then she had buried the calf beneath the doorstep—all of which was so old and powerful a form of magic that she was afraid to confess to it, in case other people got to hear of it and accused her for a witch. She was certain it would work, however, and so she continued stubborn as before.

"Never you mind what kind of a charm it was," she told Colin. "It will work—that is all you need to know. In fact—"

Anna paused, tilting her head to listen, and then finished triumphantly,

"It's working now—this very moment!"

Colin and the twins also listened—heads tilted, ears straining. True enough, the banging at the door had stopped just a second before Anna's final words, and now the Grollican's roaring was dying into an angry rumble. The noise of its footsteps going round and round the house was the next thing they heard;

then slowly the footsteps retreated in the direction of the stable, and after that there was silence.

All four of them kept perfectly still, listening to this silence, feeling the blessed peace of it. Then at last, Anna stirred, and broke the spell of this peace.

"And it's dawn, too," said she, glancing at the grey light outside the window. "The night is really over, Colin. It's over, and we have won!"

"And so it's finally safe to let you free," added Hector, beginning to untie Colin's bonds.

"We're all safe now," Hugh said thankfully, "although it seemed a near thing for a while—especially when the Grollican started banging on the door!"

There was a lot more chatter like this while the twins finished untying Colin, and although he was stiff and sore when he finally got to his feet, he was as cheerful as they were. Hugh went outside then, to get some eggs for the breakfast. Hector ran upstairs to waken Ian, and as soon as this had left Colin and Anna on their own, Colin turned to her and asked,

"Well, girl? Am I forgiven now?"

"Oh," said Anna, "I think so—providing you promise never to see hide or hair of that fairy woman again!"

"Gladly!" exclaimed Colin. "I never had anything but trouble because of her. And she is nothing at all to me now that you have broken the spell she put on me."

"Then you are forgiven," Anna agreed; at which, Colin laughed, and hugged her.

"You were right," said he, when they had finished making up the last of their quarrel. "This time we really have won against the Grollican; because I swear to you, Anna, that never again will I be deceived into letting the creature cause trouble between you and me."

Anna was given no time to answer this before the twins came back into the kitchen—Hugh walking cautiously as he balanced some new-laid eggs in his hands, but Hector fairly dashing in, with a face of great alarm on him.

"It's Ian," said he, not waiting to be asked what was wrong. "He's not upstairs. And what's more, his bed was not slept in at all last night."

All the others gaped at this news. Then Anna let out a cry, and clapped her hands to her face.

"Of course!" she exclaimed. "You all know what he's like with the little brown filly! He has to be torn away from her, almost, and I remember now he just didn't answer when I called him in from the stable last night. I forgot about him then, what with everything else that was happening . . ."

Anna did not finish what she had been going to say. Nor was there any need for her to do so, because the meaning of it was already plain to them all.

It was not only Anna who had forgotten Ian. They had all done so; and Ian, of course, had seized on this as the chance to fulfil his wish of sleeping beside the little brown filly, in the stable. But that same chance had only happened because of the Grollican; and as it prowled around that night, the Grollican had been angry—seeking revenge. Even worse, when it had departed at last, it was in the direction of the stable it had gone!

Colin felt his scalp crawl with horror at the thought of the danger this might have spelt for Ian lying, all unsuspecting, asleep in the straw there, and a look at the others showed him the same feeling mirrored in their faces. Too upset now to trust his tongue with speech, he nodded in the direction of the stable; and quickly, in the same silent dread of what they might find there, the whole family followed as he ran towards it.

7 *The Bad Wild Eyes*

WHEN COLIN and the others came rushing into the stable, the first thing they saw there was the little brown filly.

She was lying down, with her head turned towards the opening door, and her eyes gleamed in the shaft of light that fell through it. Then Colin flung the door wide open, the dimness in the rest of the stable suddenly became all light, and they saw Ian lying curled up against her side.

Ian was fast asleep, and breathing as peacefully as he had ever done in his own bed; but the filly moved at the sudden opening of the door, and the moment this happened he was wide awake and staring up at all the faces bending over him.

"There's not a mark on him," said Anna, and her voice shook with the relief of knowing this.

Colin glanced all around the stable, noting that everything there was in its usual order. Also, the only other creature to be seen there was Dondo, the old hill pony that was the general beast of burden around the croft; but it was only when he had made quite sure of this that Colin added,

"And not a sign of the Grollican!"

Anna had pulled Ian to his feet by that time and was scolding him heartily, the way a mother always does when one of her children has worried her; but Ian himself was quite bewildered by all the fuss, even although he knew he deserved a telling-off for not having come when he was called. He clung to the little brown filly, who was also on her feet by then, and Colin could not help noticing the comfort he seemed to draw from her.

"I was troubled by the Grollican last night," said he, breaking into Anna's angry words. "That's why we worried about you."

"Well, you needn't have done," Ian told him. "The creature wouldn't harm me, would it? And surely to goodness it would never harm the filly!"

Colin shook his head, not knowing what to say to this. Certainly, he thought, they had all been right to fear that the Grollican would turn its anger on Ian. But could it be so truly wicked as to harm the boy—*really* harm him? As for the filly, she was such a gentle little creature that he could not help fearing for her too; yet despite this, he still had the oddest feeling that nothing could happen to Ian so long as he was with her. It was maybe something to do with that wise look in her eyes, Colin told himself. But whatever it was, it still gave him this strange feeling that she could and indeed *would* protect Ian from all harm.

"Just you do as your mother tells you in future," said he, not wanting to speak of these thoughts at the time. But once they were all safely back in the house again and all the fuss had died down, he did tell Anna about them.

"Imagination!" Anna exclaimed. "You always did have too much imagination, Colin, and Ian is just the same. What's more, the filly is only a little creature, but the Grollican is huge. And so how could she protect Ian against it?"

"I don't know," Colin admitted. "But anyone can see that Ian and she are fond of one another, and the fairy magic on her has made her strong. Also, the Grollican fears the fairy people

—I saw it run from them, remember? And so I think that may-be it fears their magic too."

"Don't put too much store on that," Anna retorted. "Maybe the Grollican ran just so that it could live to fight another day—and that day might see it revenged on the fairies for hounding it from their hall! For all we know too, it might be through the filly it means to be revenged; and at the same time, to bring more trouble on *you*!"

"Oh, it's cunning enough for that, I agree," said Colin. "But it's still Ian we're bothered about, Anna. Is the Grollican wicked enough to trouble me by trying to harm *him*?"

"We're much better to be safe than sorry over that," Anna told him. "Which means that Ian can beg as hard as he likes to sleep in the stable with the filly, but he'll never be allowed to do that again."

The argument went on for a good while after that—long enough, indeed, for Anna to win this last point. For the rest, however, she had to admit there was something in what Colin had said about the filly being able and willing to protect Ian. And so, to make up to the boy for refusing to let him stay with the filly at night, it was agreed that he would at least be given full charge of her throughout each day.

"And that means a lot to me, remember," Colin warned him, "because she can make quite good earnings for me at the ploughing, and we can do with these earnings. Just you keep that well in mind, boy, and we'll all be happy."

Ian promised to remember all this. "And I promise again," said he, "that I'll make sure she is never yoked to anything except a plough."

"It's a bargain then," Colin agreed, and went off to catch up on all the sleep he had lost. The next day he was back at work in the forest as usual; and as usual, he was on the lookout for any trouble the Grollican might cause him. He took a vow to himself, too, that he would try not to lose his temper at anything which might happen. But the bad habits of a lifetime are not conquered in a day, of course, and he roared with rage when his axe-handle suddenly snapped in his grip and he discovered that this was because the Grollican had sawn half-way through it.

"But I'll do better another time," he promised himself. And the next day, when he found that the Grollican had tangled up all the ropes he used for hauling timber, he did none of his usual shouting and swearing. Instead, he whipped off his bonnet; and, standing bare-headed like this, he closed his eyes and prayed rapidly aloud,

"O Lord, help me to keep my temper. O Lord, help me to keep my temper. O LORD, HELP ME TO KEEP MY *TEMPER!*"

Fairly roaring at the Lord, he was, by the third time of saying; but at least, he thought, he had tried. And surely that was something? What was more, he would keep on trying until he had made the Grollican laugh on the other side of its ugly face. And surely also, then, once it had found there was no more pleasure to be had out of troubling him, he would be rid of it at last?

So Colin reasoned to himself; and so, with more or less success each time, he kept on trying not to lose his temper. The twins noticed the change that was taking place in him, and said—disrespectfully, of course, as growing boys often talk of their father,

"The old man is learning sense at last!"

Anna also noticed the change, and was very touched by it; but even so, she could not resist the chance to improve the occasion.

"It's terrible indeed," said she, "that you should be plagued by a wicked one like the Grollican, and I would be the first to admit that. But you might find it all worthwhile in the end, Colin, if it teaches you to curb your temper, because that is the wicked one within yourself. And it's the wicked one within you, my lad, which is your real enemy."

Colin felt annoyed at being preached over like this, but he fought against that feeling. Nor did he speak a word to Anna about it, because he could see that she meant no offence. Also, he was just beginning to realise that no ordinary person can ever tell just what will make a touchy man flare up in anger.

"You could be right," said he, grinding his teeth in the effort not to roar the words at her. And both Anna and the twins were delighted by this peaceable answer. So far as Ian was concerned, however, most of this simply passed him by, Colin always having been gentle with him at least, in the past. Besides which, he was much too taken up with the little brown filly to bother thinking at all about the Grollican; and as for the filly herself, she seemed to be as much taken up with him.

The first thing Ian did every morning was to loose her from the stable, and wherever he went after that, she followed him the way a faithful dog will trot to heel. She was there behind him when he went about his work of tending the animals on the croft, and soon the lambs, the chickens, the calves, and all the other creatures there had given her the same trust they gave him.

She would take food and water only from his hand; and watching the two of them together like this, Colin would have sworn she understood every word Ian said to her.

The filly was there too, when Ian's work was finished and he was free to go roaming over the hills, which was something he loved to do. Off the two of them would start, then, the filly trotting by his side and he with his arm around her neck. And that would be the last anyone saw of them till they came home in the mouth of the night, with Ian's steps dragging a bit by then, but his arm still around the creature's neck. The filly herself would be stepping neat and light as always, and looking like a small, strange princess in the crown of flowers Ian had picked for her to wear.

At times, in fact, when Colin saw them coming home like this, he used to find himself wondering if she really could be some sort of princess. Then he would tell himself that this was a very far-fetched idea, because how could the fairies have put such a person under their magic when there was no princess living within seven hundred miles of the glen?

All the same, he had to admit to himself that it was not natural for a creature like a filly to have as much sense as she had. And it was not natural, either, for her to have that look of understanding in her eyes. It could very well be the case, he thought, that the fairies had magicked some other person—someone, perhaps who was not so high-born as a princess—into the shape of a little brown filly. But whether or not that was the case, it would be foolish not to take advantage of what she could do for them all in the way of ploughing.

So Colin set about the business of hiring the filly to work on other crofts, as well as on his own; and it was Ian, of course, who was trusted with the job of taking her out in the morning, and bringing her back when the work was finished. This he did as faithfully as he did all his other work, and was always careful to see that no one took advantage of her because of her size.

"Come on, my good brown lass," he would coax each time he set out with her. And each time when he was ready to come home again, he would tell her, "That's my clever lass!"

It would never do to call her by any other name, he used to think, because she must already have been given a name sometime, somewhere, before the magic was put on her; and it would be a shame to confuse her now with a new one.

"Ian's lass," was the name other people gave her as a result of this, and the name stuck; so that, very soon, she was "Ian's lass" to everyone else in the glen. The natural scorn at her small size did not last, either—not once they saw what she could do and heard the reason for her powers. The wonder and amazement at all this started a great clamour for her services; and although these glen folk were all crofters with no spare money to command, they were all willing to pay in kind, with potatoes, or barley, or flour and other useful things.

The Grant family began to live very well out of these payments, and Colin found this helped him to keep his temper when the Grollican troubled him—because it is much easier, after all, to be good-natured on a full stomach than on an empty one. Also both he and Anna were pleased with the way Ian took care of the filly, which made them proud of the name "Ian's lass". And as for the twins, their hearts were too generous for them to be jealous of the fame their young brother was getting for himself.

"We're big and strong," said Hugh. "We'll always be able to make a living for ourselves. But Ian has a crooked shoulder; and forby, he is only a wee lad."

"Aye," Hector took up the story. "He needs something extra to make up for all that, and it's fine he is getting such pleasure from the filly."

The two of them were busy repairing a fence when they spoke like this. Their heads were down to the work, and neither of them saw the big, grey shape of the Grollican flitting past them. Anna was in the house at the time. Colin was miles away in the forest. Not one of them even suspected the creature was near, or that it was up to its tricks again—although Colin and

Anna, at least, should have remembered that a man who is troubled by the Grollican is always in greatest danger just when matters are going well with him; this being the very time when the Grollican delights in using its wicked ways to spoil such a state of affairs. And for Colin at that particular time, of course, all the work the filly had been hired to do meant that matters were indeed going well.

It was not Colin himself however, that the Grollican had in mind that day. It was Ian, who happened to be in the stable with the little brown filly. They were lying in the straw, the two of them, resting from their day's work, and Ian was talking away to the filly as he usually did on these occasions. He never got an answer from her, of course, but it was still something he liked to do, simply because he had no one of his own age to speak to—which meant there were a lot of things in his mind he never otherwise got a chance to say. Besides this, he had the feeling that the little brown filly understood these things.

He was blethering on in this way, then, flat on his back in the straw and staring up to the rafters of the stable roof, when suddenly he realised he could see a pair of eyes. There was no face around the eyes, and no body of any thing or any person— just the eyes themselves looking down from about eight feet above the floor of the stable. And that was strange enough, but there was something stranger yet about all this.

In the first place, the eyes were huge and completely round in shape. There was something bad and wild in the look of them; and yet, behind the wickedness there was also a kind of sadness—a very odd kind of sadness which was almost as if the creature that owned the eyes was pleading people to understand that the badness and wildness were none of its own fault.

Ian lay quite still for a moment, trying to get over the shock of seeing those eyes, and then his mind began working very quickly, remembering everything that had happened since the day Colin had come home from the woods with the hole in his bonnet. He was a clever boy, Ian, and even although his father had seen to it that no one had spoken much to him of these things, he had thought about them for himself. In a flash, then, he put two and two together, and guessed that the eyes looking down at him were those of the Grollican.

Now it has to be remembered at this point that, from the very beginning, Ian had felt sorry for the Grollican. He still felt it was a shame for the creature to be so ugly it would not show itself, and so he was not frightened to find himself suddenly alone with it in the stable. Also, the filly was showing no signs of fright, and this made him feel that the Grollican meant him no harm. He was curious about it, all the same; added to which he wanted to make certain that the eyes did indeed belong to that creature. And so, looking straight up to them, he asked,

"Is that the Grollican there?"

The eyes moved, down and then up, as if the Grollican had nodded its head.

"Can you speak?" Ian asked then.

There was a silence for a moment; and then, from the place where the eyes were, a voice said,

"If I want to."

The voice was a very ugly one, harsh and loud, with a growling note in it; but Ian thought it was a step forward that the Grollican had consented to answer at all, and so he was quite pleased to hear this voice.

"Will you show yourself to me?" he asked.

There was another silence, and then, from the Grollican, a loud "No!"

"Why not?" asked Ian, and this time the answer came quickly.

"I'm ugly!"

"That's no reason—" Ian began, but the Grollican interrupted,

"Yes it is. People hate ugly things.'

"Not everybody hates ugly things," Ian argued. "I don't, for one."

"You'll hate me, I'm the ugliest thing in the Otherworld," the Grollican said sourly. But even as it spoke, Ian began to see the shape of a face forming vaguely around the eyes. He kept his own features still, pretending not to have noticed anything, and said encouragingly,

"But there are ugly things in this world too, you know, and I don't hate them."

The shape of the Grollican's face grew clearer when he said this, and so he went on,

"Frogs, for instance—they're ugly enough, goodness knows, but I don't hate frogs. I like them!"

By this time he could really see the Grollican's face, with its flat nose and its thick lips that had two long fangs sprouting from under the upper one. He could also see its furry grey head and the two pointed ears that stuck up from it, and the sight was indeed such an ugly one that he had a job not to gape at it. The Grollican scowled at him, and clashed its fangs with a horrible sound.

"What d'ye think of me, then?" it snarled. "What d'ye think, eh?"

"It's not your fault that you're ugly," Ian told it. "That's what I think for the moment, at least."

The shape of the Grollican's body appeared suddenly, all eight feet of it as grey and furry as its head. There was a hump on its huge shoulders, and its clumsy, three-toed feet were covered with warts. It had four arms, two growing from its shoulders, and two growing from its chest; and at the end of each one there was a great hairy hand with six fingers on it.

"NOW!" it challenged again, bellowing the word at the top of its harsh voice. "*Now* do you like me?"

Ian's breath had come out in a great gasp when he saw the full ugliness of the Grollican; and after the first glance, he turned his face away to bury it in the mane of the little brown filly. He was terribly frightened now, he had to admit that; but the silky feel of the filly's mane was comforting, and so was the velvety touch of her nose nuzzling gently against his hand.

No harm could come to him while he was with her, he thought. She was fond of him, and she would use the magic that was on her to protect him from the Grollican. That was what his father had told him, and he believed it was true. Slowly he looked up at the terrible apparition in front of him.

"There is a magic on the filly that makes her strong," he said quietly, "and she understands every word I say. She will protect me."

"I know all that," the Grollican snarled. "Being ugly doesn't mean I'm stupid as well, you know. But I never said I'd harm you, did I?"

"No," agreed Ian, taking courage from this answer. "But something else you never said was why you came here in the first place."

"Mind your own business," the Grollican said rudely, "and I'll mind mine. And answer a question when it's put to you, if you don't mind."

"About liking you, you mean?" Ian asked, and tried to think what he should say next. The Grollican waited, clashing its fangs every so often, and at last Ian said cautiously,

"Well, you haven't given me any cause to like you, so far. But

I certainly don't hate you because you're ugly. In fact, I—I feel sorry for you."

The Grollican stopped clashing its fangs. The bad, wild look suddenly went out of its eyes, and the strange sadness Ian had noticed filled them instead. The sad eyes looked down, wandering all over its great, misshapen form, and piteously it said,

"You don't know what it's like, carrying such an ugly body around all the time."

The pity Ian felt for the Grollican had been deep down in his heart till that moment, but now he could feel it welling up like a full, clear spring rising strongly from the dark earth to the light of day. The feeling made him so breathless he could hardly form the words he wanted to speak, but at last he managed to say,

"No, I don't know. But I can guess what it's like because, you see, I'm—well, I'm a bit twisted myself."

With that, he turned so that the Grollican had a good view of his crooked shoulder. "And I was born like this," he added, glancing up and over his shoulder; and grudgingly the Grollican said,

"Och, well, that was bad luck, right enough. But it's still only a wee hump you've got, not a great big one like mine."

"It fits my size," said Ian, "the same as your hump fits your size. And you don't hear me complaining about mine, do you? What's more I don't think that the way I feel about having it gives me the right to make a nuisance of myself like you do."

"Aye, but—" said the Grollican, with the bad wild look coming back into its eyes. "Aye, but—"

And so the two of them went on arguing about this, with Ian insisting that the Grollican had no business to be going around troubling people just so that it could get out its spite over being ugly, while the Grollican roared the opposite. And when it looked as if Ian might get the better of the argument, the way it finished was that the Grollican simply disappeared from his sight altogether.

It was no longer anywhere in the stable, either, Ian realised once he had discovered he was talking to empty air, and had felt all around to discover whether he could touch it, even if he could no longer see it. All of which took quite a bit of time, because he had first to summon enough courage to face the thought of laying a hand on the Grollican. Once he had concluded it was gone, however, he felt oddly disappointed; and this feeling grew stronger when he remembered the look of sadness the Grollican had worn at its own ugliness.

If only, he told himself—if only the Grollican had given him a little more time to talk before it disappeared! He was certain he could have won the argument, if that had been the case. But even so, he decided in the end, the mere fact of the argument itself seemed to prove that the Grollican did indeed have a conscience over the damage it did. Also the things it had said to him when it was starting to let itself be seen, seemed to show that all it really wanted was to have a little liking from people. And if it could not have that because of its ugliness, it was indeed a creature more to be pitied than blamed for its wicked ways.

Ian went off to the house thinking of all these things, and telling himself what they finally proved. He himself had been right all along about the Grollican, and his father had been wrong. He still knew very well, however, that he would never be able to convince his father of this. Also, if he admitted he had actually seen and talked to the Grollican, his father would be afraid for him—which meant he might find himself being kept strictly to the house, in case the Grollican paid him another visit.

Being a house-bound prisoner was the very last thing Ian wanted to risk, because that would spell an end to all his jaunts with the little brown filly. Also—although he had not much hope that this would happen—he was anxious to see if the Grollican would come to talk to him again. And so, by the time he came in at the door that night, he had decided to take what seemed to him the much smaller risk of keeping altogether silent on his first experience of it.

"You're very quiet, all of a sudden," Anna said to him that night. "Has the cat got your tongue?"

"He's thinking of the little brown filly," said Colin, smiling. "That's what he's got on his mind."

"No it's not," Hector teased. "It's the thought of the Grollican that's bothering him."

Both Hugh and Hector laughed at this but Colin said sharply,

"That's enough! I told you I didn't want Ian frightened by talk of the Grollican."

"I'm not frightened, Da," said Ian; but that was all he said, even although this was a good chance to start telling of what had happened that day.

Afterwards also, he thought he had reason to congratulate himself on sticking to the decision not to talk about it, because it so happened that the Grollican did appear in the stable again. Not once, either, but quite a number of times; so that he grew quite used to talking to it and to seeing its face and form gradually becoming visible.

The talk was mostly argument, mind you, the very same kind of argument that had gone on at its first visit; and whenever it looked as if Ian would win this argument, the Grollican simply disappeared as it had then. Ian had nothing of his father's quick temper in him, however, and so he never flared up in annoyance over this.

What he did instead was simply to wait for his next chance to use the good, sharp mind God had given him, and in this way he managed to get the Grollican to talk quite a bit about itself. Very soon then, he discovered it was a terrible boaster, which gave him the opportunity to have a really hard dig at it one day, because the thing it boasted about oftener than anything else was its great, its really enormous strength.

"If you're really all that strong," said Ian that day, "why do you not use some of your strength to work for people instead of troubling them? That's what you would do, you know, if you truly wanted them to begin liking you."

"No!" shouted the Grollican. "Why should I have to work just to make people like me? It's not my fault, I've told you that. It's not my fault I'm ugly!"

With this, it made itself invisible again, still shouting "Ugly ... ugly ..." until the sound of its voice dying eerily away told Ian it had gone altogether from the stable. It still came back a few days later, all the same, and although he knew he could never want to do more than glance at anything so horrid, he was pleased by this. Indeed he realised then, he had got to the point where he was no longer just sorry for the creature. In a queer sort of way, he was actually beginning to like it, and he had the feeling that the Grollican also realised this.

Gradually, from that time, it began to speak to him in a gentler voice. Gradually too, they stopped arguing so much, and began to exchange odds and ends of conversation instead. Ian began to think from all this that the Grollican was finally making the effort to be friendly with him; and in these thoughts, as it happened, he was absolutely right.

What Ian could not know, however, was that it had no intention of allowing the friendliness to distract it from its first purpose in coming to the stable. Also, it was determined that he should never guess at this purpose; and so, whenever he ventured to ask about it, he still got nothing but rudeness in reply.

Even so, Ian was now so certain the Grollican would never harm him that he could not believe it had first come to the stable with any bad intent; but this belief, as it also happened, was absolutely wrong. There came a day, then, when his talk with the Grollican was on very different lines from everything that had gone before, and he discovered at last the real reason for the first and every other visit the creature had paid him.

8 The Great Decision

It was late in the afternoon of that day, and Ian had just led the little brown filly into the stable. As it happened, too, he was all alone on the croft. The twins were away up the hill with the old pony Dondo, collecting a load of peats. Colin was far away in the forest. Anna had gone to visit a friend who lived further west along the glen.

The Grollican appeared, as suddenly as it always did, and the first thing it said was,

"There's a sheep in trouble a mile down the road there. All tangled up in a bramble-bush, it is, and one of its legs is broken."

"I'll have to bring it home then," said Ian in dismay. "But how? I'll never be able to carry a sheep all that distance."

"You don't have to carry it," the Grollican said impatiently. "Use a wagon—a cart—anything with wheels. There's a little cart in the yard there that would just suit the purpose."

"I know," cried Ian. "But it's still too heavy for me to pull, and my brothers have taken Dondo off to haul a load of peats for the fire."

"Use the filly then," the Grollican told him. "She's strong enough, according to all you say."

"But the filly must never be yoked to anything except a plough," Ian protested, "or else all the magic will go from her. And I've twice promised my father I would never allow that to happen."

"Then it's just bad luck for the sheep, isn't it?" said the

Grollican, and gave a shrug that dismissed any further interest in the matter.

Ian stood wondering what to do, then awkwardly, he said, "You're strong. You could pull the cart for me."

The Grollican glared at him. "You've got your nerve, boy!" it roared. "Why should *I* make myself a beast of burden?"

"To help me, that's why," Ian told it. "I need help if I'm to bring that sheep home, but my father's in the forest, my brothers are miles away up the hill, and my mother's gone west the glen on a visit. And so there's no one here I can ask—except you."

Now the truth of this whole matter was that the Grollican had planned for it to happen in exactly the way it was happening.

First of all it had won Ian's confidence with its visits to the stable. Then it had waited for a day when he would be alone on the croft before it appeared with its lying story about the sheep —because this was all a lie, of course. The Grollican had made it up as it lurked about that day, watching all the other members of the family go their separate ways, and it had chosen this sort of lie because it knew how tender-hearted Ian was to all animals. Also, the purpose of the lie was to trouble Colin still further by persuading Ian to yoke the little brown filly to something other than a plough, and so take all the magic from her.

It still had to be very careful to hide this purpose from Ian, however; and so now it pretended to forget its anger and very cunningly instead, it argued,

"The sheep is in a bad enough state as it is, but it might be even worse if I go near it. Indeed, I wouldn't be surprised if the creature died of the fright it would get. And who would be to blame for that but you."

Ian bit his lip in great distress at this, because he knew very well that a sheep with a broken leg and its fleece all tangled in thorny trails of bramble, must be suffering great pain; and even if it did not die, but only struggled at the sight of the Grollican, that pain would become terrible indeed.

"You needn't let it see you," he suggested, but the Grollican only retorted,

"And how would that help, when it could still scent me?"

"Then what am I to do?" Ian asked. "I can't let it lie there suffering until my father or the twins come home, and so what *am* I to do?"

"Please yourself on that," the Grollican told him. "You've got the filly here, and you've got a cart she can pull; but if you're too stubborn to yoke her to the cart, that's your affair. Besides which, I've already done enough by telling you about the sheep to begin with—although it's small thanks I seem to have got for it!"

With a final glare of its bad, wild eyes, it began to disappear from Ian's sight; and in sudden panic at this, he shouted,

"Wait, Grollican—wait a moment!"

The Grollican came back to its full shape, and Ian went on,

"How could you tell the sheep had a broken leg?"

"Because I saw the queer way that leg hung from the creature's body," the Grollican said cruelly.

Ian felt himself go white at this. "And was it making much of a struggle to get free of the bramble bush?" he asked.

"Aye, and bawling its head off with the pain," the Grollican told him—enjoying itself now!

Ian gasped, and felt he was going to be sick; yet still it was the very cruelty of the Grollican's words that made up his mind for him. He could not leave the sheep in pain like that, he decided; and since there was no other way to rescue it, he had no choice now except to yoke the filly to the cart. And supposing that *did* mean breaking his promise? Supposing it *did* mean the filly would lose her magic? Any half-decent person would agree, surely, that no amount of magic was worth another moment of such suffering for a poor, dumb creature!

Feeling sure then that he was doing the right thing, Ian led the filly out of the stable and into the yard. In trembling haste he backed her between the shafts of the cart standing there, but while he was fastening the last buckle of the harness that held her to it, he remembered he would need a knife to cut the sheep free and a rope to help him hoist it on to the cart. Straightaway, then, he ran to get these things from the stable. The Grollican was no longer there when he came running in, but Ian did not bother about that. He grabbed the rope and the knife and rushed outside with them—only to get the greatest shock he had ever had in his life.

The cart stood where he had left it, but the little brown filly was no longer between its shafts. These shafts were now lowered to the ground. The harness he had put on the filly lay between them, with all its fastenings still firmly in place, but the filly herself was gone—vanished as if she had never existed.

Ian could not believe his eyes. He called her, dashed hither and thither looking for her, still calling, at the top of his voice. Still the filly was not to be seen, not a glimpse or sign of her, and Ian had at last to accept this. What was more, he had to accept that she had vanished because he had yoked her to something other than a plough, and so had broken the magic on her. There could be no other explanation for anything so mysterious, he realised, and felt a terrible despair at his own foolishness in never once thinking that the loss of the magic might lead to the loss of the filly herself.

With his head in his hands then, Ian sat down on one of the cart-shafts to think the situation out a bit further; and right away, he began to suspect that he had the Grollican to blame for it all—that there had not been a word of truth, in fact, in its story about the sheep. He found it hard to believe, however, that even the Grollican could be so wicked as to make up such a cruel lie; and so he decided that the first thing to do was to check if there really was a sheep caught in the brambles. If that was indeed the case, he could at least cut it free and set its broken leg in a splint; and once he had done so, he would have to go up the hill to fetch the twins with the pony and cart they were using.

With great regrets that he had not thought of all this in the first place, Ian took up the knife and the rope, then set off down the road to begin his search. His eyes were open for the little brown filly as he hurried along, but still there was no sign of her. Hunt as he would, too, he could find no sign of any trapped and injured sheep, and it was with a heart full of grief and shame that he gave up the search at last.

The shame was for his own foolishness in allowing the Grollican to trick him; because this, he realised now, was something that must have been in its mind from the very beginning. This was why it had come to the stable in the first place; and it was also the reason it had continued to do so—simply to gain his trust, so that he would believe all the lies it had planned to tell.

The grief he felt was for the loss of the little brown filly, because he had truly loved that creature, and the thought that he would never see her again in life was almost more than he could bear without the comfort of tears. Even tears, however, were no comfort to Ian in the end; and by the evening of that day, all he could do was to sit listlessly waiting for his parents and his brothers to come home.

"In the name of fortune!" Anna exclaimed when she came in and saw the white look of him, the tear-streaks on his face, and his eyes all puffed up and red with crying. "What's wrong with you, my lamb?"

"The magic on the little brown filly is broken, and it's all my fault. That's what's wrong with me," said Ian. "I yoked her to a cart, instead of a plough, and she vanished into thin air."

Anna shrieked and clasped her hands to her face in dismay, but Ian went on talking, trying to explain to her how it had all happened. The twins came home in the middle of this, with Colin hard on their heels, so that Ian had to go right back to the beginning of his story; and the moment he had confessed about the way the filly had vanished, Colin's face became black as thunder. Such a rage boiled up in him, indeed, that he could hardly speak; and before he could manage to shape a single word, Ian said,

"You'd better just beat me and get it over with, Da. I know this is one time when you have a real right to lose your temper."

Rage was still holding Colin speechless—or nearly so. But he was still a man who would rather have all the seas of the world wash over his head than be cruel to a child, and anger did not stop him realising that it would be cruelty indeed to lay hands on such a pitiful figure as Ian was then. He took one final look at the white and tear-stained face.

"I'll be back," said he, and rushed outside, into the yard. There he stood for several moments letting his rage burst from him in a great roar and shaking both fists up towards the sky. Then he danced around, yelling and cursing till his throat was sore, after which he felt he was ready to listen more peaceably to anything else Ian had to say.

"Let's hear what excuse you have, then," said he, coming back into the house.

Ian carried on with what he had to say, starting this time at the true beginning of his story, telling every detail of what had happened between himself and the Grollican, and also giving the conclusions he had drawn from all this. Colin and the others heard him out in silence, and when he was finished at last, he told Colin,

"That's all, Da. And—and I'm sorry, Da."

"'Sorry' won't bring the little brown filly back," Colin said bitterly. "But you can stop blaming yourself, son, because I don't blame you. You were no match for anything so cunning as the Grollican—that was the whole trouble. But you weren't to know that, of course. How could you, a lad of your age?"

With anger flushing red in his face again, he looked around the others and told them,

"All the same, this settles it! This trick that has robbed me of the filly is the very last bit of trouble the Grollican will bring on me, because I'll live no longer at the mercy of its spite."

"But what choice have you?" asked Anna, wringing her hands in distress.

"I have this choice," Colin told her. "I can leave this glen, leave the country altogether, in fact. I can emigrate—go from here to another country, where the Grollican will not follow me."

The twins stood aghast at this, and so did Ian, but Anna was not nearly so put out as some wives would have been. It was not the first time she had heard talk of emigrating, after all, and she had already seen plenty of her own folk go off to foreign lands—this having long been the way of things among Scottish people. Colin's words still gave her plenty to think about, however, and so now she asked,

"But if you emigrated, Colin, where would you go? Where would *we* go—because we would have to go with you, of course, if you did leave this country."

The twins both started to speak at once then, but Colin hushed them down.

"I'll tell you where," said he. "We'll go to America. That's where my cousin Hamish went, when he emigrated—indeed, there's half the people in the glen have kin-folk in that country. And besides, it's far enough away from here to fool even the Grollican."

"I'm not going to America," said the twins in one breath.

Colin swung round on them. "You'll do as I say," he roared. "And I say we're going to put an ocean between me and the Grollican, because that's the only way I'll ever get rid of it."

"You can't be sure of that," Anna protested; but Colin retorted,

"Of course I can. When did you ever hear of the Grollican in America?"

Anna had no answer to this, of course, because no creature of the Otherworld is ever heard of in a modern country like America. The twins still had plenty to say, however, and it was Hector who spoke next.

"You must do as you think best for yourself," he told Colin, "but you still have to understand that there's always one who wants to stay in this country for every one who wants to leave it. That's how it has always been, Da; and that's why I won't follow you to America or anywhere else. I'm one of those who must stay here in my own land, because that land is in my blood and in my bones, and I cannot live without it."

"That's how I feel too, Da," Hugh said quietly. "There are some plants that cannot put down roots in new soil, you know; and if I was torn from the roots I've grown in this country, I would be like one of those plants. I would wither and die for lack of the shape and feel of my own land around me."

Never before had Colin heard his twin sons speak at such

length, or with such feeling. Indeed, the fact that they were not clever lads had led him into the mistake of thinking that they did not have any really deep feelings—a very common mistake, as it happens, and many another person like the twins could have told him so. He was a just man, however, and now that his eyes were open to his error, his imagination began to tell him all that these two had left unspoken.

He looked at Anna. She looked back at him, and each of them knew what the other was thinking. Wherever Hugh and Hector went, they would carry with them a vision of mountains, and wide ever-changing Highland skies. They would see those mountains purple with heather, or starred by the small, pale primroses of Spring—or maybe, again, with the shapes of cattle outlined against the sky when the mountain tops stood dark in the mouth of the night.

They would see the little white houses of the glen crouching in sheltered hollows, the brown peaty streams of mountain water rushing fast over rocky river-beds. And always, always, *always*, they would long for the vision of these things to be there, in very truth, before their eyes.

"We must leave them free to choose," Colin said quietly to Anna at last. And to the twins, he said, "Well, boys, stay if you must. We'll miss you, but we understand your decision, and we'll not blame you for it."

The twins looked relieved at this, but they were very solemn also. As for Anna, she was now clearly upset at the thought of her own part in the situation.

"But what about me?" she asked. "How can *I* go to a strange country, leaving two of my sons behind me?"

"Those two sons are almost grown men," Colin pointed out. "They will be looking around for wives in a year or two, and then they would be leaving you to set up homes of their own."

"It's all the worse for me that they're grown," cried Anna. "They'll soon be having children of their own; and if I'm in America, that means I'll have grandchildren I'll never be able to dandle on my knee!"

"You have another son to get you grandchildren," Colin reminded her. "Wait till Ian's grown and takes a wife to himself. You'll dandle grandchildren then to your heart's content."

Anna looked at Ian, and forgot to argue further. "That lad's for his bed!" she announced. "He's half-dead with tiredness and the strain of all these goings-on."

This was true, indeed, and so Ian was packed off to his bed where he lay thinking he would never sleep for grieving after the little brown filly and wondering what had happened to her. His mind was tired, however, as well as his body. He was asleep before he knew it, while downstairs the discussion about going to America went on late into the night.

The twins, it was decided, would take over the croft between them, and each of them would also try for a job in the forestry.

"That way, you'll manage fine," Colin told them. "But when you come to marry, be sure to choose a girl that has a bit of land to her name, and then you can each have a croft to work. Furthermore, the Head Forester is a good man and he thinks well of me. I can easily persuade him to give work to both of you."

"And while you're doing that," Anna told Colin, "I'll write to your cousin Hamish—him that's already emigrated to America —just to let him know we'll be joining him there."

Anna wrote a good hand, the best in the family; and what was more, Colin knew that his cousin would be glad to see him.

"Aye, you do that," he agreed. "And I'll go into the town and sell my watch to help raise the fare."

"We'll need more than the price of a silver watch to go all the way to New York," said Anna, because it was to New York they would have to go first of all before they travelled on another fifty miles to where Colin's cousin stayed.

So they went on discussing one problem after another, sometimes finding an answer, and sometimes leaving the problem to be solved another day. There were some things, too, that Colin had to take advice on from friends who also had relatives in America. And once he had done so, it was not long after that first discussion that the whole glen knew of the plans for Colin, Anna, and Ian to emigrate to that country.

"And what will you do in America?" people began to ask him.

"I'll farm, of course, the same as I do here," was Colin's answer.

"Aye, that would be the right thing," they agreed. "And your cousin Hamish—would he help you to get the land for that, do you suppose?"

"If he doesn't," said Colin, "then he's no cousin of mine any more!"

"Yes, yes," said they. "Blood's thicker than water, to be sure. But you mightn't like the living in these foreign parts, Colin. And the family mightn't like it either.'

"Yes they will," Colin insisted. "And so will I. We couldn't make ends meet here, after all, unless I had a job in the forestry. But they have much bigger farms in America than we have here, which will mean a better living for all of us. And who wouldn't like that?"

This was a good argument that convinced some, although it didn't quite convince others. But one and all, when they understood the reason behind the move, they agreed it was still the only way that Colin could hope to escape from the Grollican.

No one thought of asking Ian what he felt about leaving the glen, of course, since it was taken for granted that a boy of his age would prefer to be where his parents were, and that he would always do as he was told in any case. Also, Ian himself never spoke a word on the subject, even although he secretly hated the thought of leaving the glen without knowing what had happened to the little brown filly.

Secretly too, he kept hoping he might find her back on the croft one day, as suddenly as she had vanished from it. Nor could he entirely forget the deep and terrible sadness that had seemed to lie behind the bad, wild look in the eyes of the Grollican, and so he had one other secret hope. Perhaps, he thought, that creature knew where the filly was; and perhaps it would regret its wickedness enough to tell him how to find her.

Now the Grollican, as it happened, was indeed uneasy over the cruel way it had taken advantage of Ian. Deep down in its wicked mind, too, it was sorry it had thrown away the chance of friendship with him. In spite of this, however, it could not help feeling pleased at having pulled off a trick which had not only troubled Colin, but had given it revenge on the fairies into the bargain.

All this meant it had not the least intention of telling Ian where the filly was, or listening to any reproaches he might feel like making. On the contrary, it was careful to stay invisible to him; and in this form, it went back to its old habit of making a nuisance of itself to Colin in small ways, until it could think of some other really disastrous trouble to bring on him.

After a while, then, Ian began to realise that nothing would or could be done about the filly unless he did it himself. It occurred to him also, that the filly might not be able to come back to him, however willing she was to do that. And so, while all the rest of the family went on talking of the move to

America and laying further plans for this, he began making a great search for her.

He had no difficulty either in adding the fact of this search to his store of secrets. Indeed, he had always been so much in the habit of roaming alone in the hills that no one thought to question the way he took to disappearing for hours at a time on this new ploy. Day after day, therefore, he went up one hill path and down another in search of the filly. Over moors he went too, through forest and across rivers; searching, always searching. A small figure he was, in the great loneliness of these places, but a stubborn one too, with his one crooked shoulder held higher than the other and his eyes forever peering ahead to catch some sudden glimpse of his beloved filly.

Curiously enough, however, it made no difference in the end how far he roamed or what byways he followed, because he nearly always found himself heading for home by way of a certain big, open space in a wood some five miles west of his own house. Whenever he did this, too, he remembered that every time he had left the little brown filly to choose the path in the days they had gone wandering together, she also had headed for this same open space. This had puzzled him at the time. It puzzled him now to think why *he* should persist in going back to it, and there was many a day when he stood looking around it for some answer to the puzzle.

It was high up on the hillside, this open space, and the reason the trees had been cleared from it to begin with, was to allow a gamekeeper's cottage to be built. Ian had never known the people who lived in that cottage—besides which, there was one night a year before this time when it had gone on fire, and now there was nothing left of it but a burnt-out shell. This was something that gave the place an air of desolation which seemed to make it all the more remarkable that the filly had deliberately headed for it in the days gone past. It was strange too, Ian thought, that *he* should be drawn to such a lonely place where there was nothing to see but the burnt-out home of people he had never known.

There came a time, also, when Ian began to wonder even more about this clearing in the woods because, as he stood at the edge of it one day, he had the feeling of being watched. He looked all around, seeing nothing at first and then suddenly catching a glimpse of a face among the trees at the far side of the clearing. The face seemed to be that of someone who was about the same age as himself, yet this someone turned and ran when he called out a greeting, and there were several occasions after that when the same thing happened to him.

He would get the feeling of being watched as he stood at the edge of the clearing, and catch a glimpse of the face peering out from the trees at its further side. Then he would call out, the face would disappear instantly, and for a moment or two he would hear the sound of someone running away from the clearing—running so fast, too, that he knew it would be hopeless to try to catch up.

That was all there ever was to it, and—partly because there was so little to tell—he never mentioned anything about it at home. Another reason for his silence, of course, was that he still did not want to give away the secret of his constant search for the little brown filly. It was a hopeless search—in his heart of hearts he had at last admitted this; and so to speak of it now would only have made his secret seem a foolish one.

"You're not taking much interest in going to America," Colin said to him one evening when he came back from yet another spell of searching. "It's your mother and me who've done all the packing so far, and no thanks at all to you that you see us now ready to go."

Ian looked at all the boxes and bundles piled up in the kitchen. Then he hung his head in shame to think he had been so taken up with his search and the mystery of the face in the woods that he had barely noticed the work of packing—never mind helping with it!

On the day following that one, however, there was an event which solved this mystery for him. And it was from this same event that both Colin and Anna discovered they had yet another decision to make before they really were ready to go to America.

9 Ian's Lass

A VISIT from the minister of the church up the glen was the beginning of it all.

He was a good, kindly man, this minister; a married man who liked young people but had no children of his own—which is maybe why matters fell out the way they did. Be that as it may, however, the minister came driving up to the door of Colin's house in a little carriage pulled by a sturdy hill pony. Then he came in to the house and sat for a while drinking tea and getting all the news—chief among which was that Colin had now raised enough money to pay the fares to New York. Also, the letter to his cousin Hamish had been sent well on its way, so that it appeared there was not one thing now to stop him and Anna and Ian going to America.

"So you'll soon be for the off," the minister remarked; and Colin agreed,

"Very soon now, minister. Very soon."

The minister rubbed his chin, seeming to think deeply, and at last it seemed also that he had come to some decision on his thoughts. He looked up, his eyes resting on Colin.

"Colin," said he, "I have a favour to ask of you, and it will not cost you anything in the way of money because I will put my hand into my own pocket for that."

"Speak on, minister," Colin encouraged, wondering what kind of favour this could possibly be; and got the surprise of his life when the minister said,

"Very well, Colin. Here is the favour. When you and Anna and Ian set off for America, I want you to take one other person with you, and to let that person live with you there as a member of your own family."

Both Colin and Anna gaped at this, with a look on their faces that showed they thought the minister had flown out of his senses. And then, as usual, Colin's touchy temper got the better of him.

"Of all the nerve, minister!" he exploded. "Am I hearing you right? And do you not think I've been troubled enough already without putting another burden like this on me?"

"I know very well the trouble you've had," the minister said tartly. "But I also know the temper that's at the root of it all. And for your own good, Colin Grant, I'm telling you now that it's time you showed a little Christian patience with people, instead of bawling and roaring at them the minute they say a word to upset you."

Colin was instantly shamed by this, and had the grace to admit it. "But I truly have been trying this while past to keep my temper in check," he added; and sounded so heartily sorry for his outburst that the minister felt kinder towards him.

"Just you keep on with the effort then, Colin," he advised. "And meanwhile, to tell you what lies behind this favour I'm asking—you'll remember Willie Mackenzie, the gamekeeper that lived some five miles up the glen from here?"

Colin nodded. "Aye, of course," said he. "I used often to see him when I was in the forest."

"I suppose you must have done," the minister agreed. "And do you remember the night his house burned to the ground?"

"I remember it well," Colin answered. "Just over a year ago, it was."

"That's right," the minister told him. "And such a tragedy,

too, with poor Willie and his wife both burned to death in the flames of that fire! But I'm sure you'll remember also, Colin, that the Mackenzies had a daughter, Flora—a wee lass of around your own Ian's age. And young Flora Mackenzie was not burned in that fire, because there was no sign of her body anywhere when people finally managed to search the ruins of the house."

"That's true!" Anna chimed in at this point. "I remember it was thought at the time that the poor lass had maybe run out of the house in such a state of shock that she just wandered off on her own and got lost."

"And then stumbled into a peat bog and drowned there," Colin added. "That sort of thing has happened before, you know, when a child went wandering; and it could have happened again with Flora. Indeed, it must have done, because she has certainly never been seen by a living soul since that time."

"Yes, she has," the minister told him. "She most certainly has, and this was the way of it. Four weeks ago, it was, on a day when I happened to be walking through that big clearing in the woods where the Mackenzies used to live. I saw her then, lying unconscious beside the burnt-out shell of their house. I carried her home to my manse, and there she has stayed ever since with me and my good wife."

Both Colin and Anna were staring in astonishment by this time, and not just because of what the minister had told them. There were other things, they realised, that had been left unsaid, and it was Anna who voiced the first of these.

"So Flora Mackenzie's alive, after all," she remarked thoughtfully. "And for four weeks now she has lived in your manse without your telling a soul about it. That's right, isn't it, minister? It must be, otherwise we would already have heard you'd found her!"

"You would," the minister agreed. "Because news travels fast in the glen—but that was my very reason for keeping quiet about this piece of news! You see, young Flora either cannot or will not say where she has been for this past year. Indeed, she never talks at all if she can help it. She never smiles, either, the way a child of her age *should* smile; and the place she makes for whenever she gets the chance, is that same clearing in the woods. It's as if she is being drawn back to it, you understand— maybe because she is trying to remember what happened there. Or maybe, even, because she remembers it too well, and it has some horrid sort of fascination for her."

"Ach, the poor wee soul!" exclaimed Anna, much moved by this, and the minister nodded.

"Aye, it's sad," he sighed. "Very sad."

Colin had also been very touched by this latest part of the minister's story, but he had kept his wits about him even better than Anna had done; and now it was his turn to put a question.

"But, minister," said he, "that's still no reason, is it, for hiding the bairn away in your own house all this month past? It seems to me she would come all the quicker back to normal if she was not kept close, but allowed out to play with other bairns her own age."

"I haven't finished the tale yet," was the minister's answer to this. "But now I will. This poor little Flora cries out in her sleep—my wife and I have both heard her—and then it's strange things she says. She mutters away about being taken into a big hall of some kind. '*All the bonnie ladies* . . .' she mutters; and, '*All that gold* . . . !' Then she begins to cry in her sleep, and to call out, '*Oh, the work! Always the work* . . . !' That's when we try to wake her to put an end to this distress. But if we leave her a while, she begins to whisper a name; and once she has done that a few times, the bad dreaming goes off her and she falls into a natural sleep."

Colin and Anna glanced swiftly at one another. Each saw the same doubt, the same question, in the other's eyes; and then, speaking low, Colin asked,

"What name is this, minister?"

The minister got up from his chair and went to look out of the window. From there, he could see Ian coming down the hill towards home, and he kept his eyes on this sight for a few moments before he turned his back to the window and said quietly,

"'Ian' is the name she whispers. Ian—always Ian."

Colin took a moment to think before he spoke again, and then he asked,

"When did you say it was, minister, this day you found her unconscious in the clearing?"

"On a Thursday, exactly four weeks ago," the minister answered, "and it was on the evening of that day. Also, as I know from having looked up the parish records, it was a Thursday when the Mackenzies' house went on fire and Flora disappeared."

Colin and Anna took yet another look at one another. Thursday, they both knew, is the day of the week when the fairy people are most likely to be abroad—indeed, in some parts of the Highlands this is so much the case that Thursday is called "fairies' day". One other thing they knew, however, was that the minister had named the very day and the very time of that day when the filly had disappeared.

There was a long silence, with all three of them wondering how to put what was now the thought in each mind. Then the minister spoke, choosing his words very carefully.

"I am a man of God," said he, "and it is my duty not to

encourage any talk of the ungodly creatures which some people believe to exist in an Otherworld. Yet still there are certain things which have to be stated fairly and openly and the business of the little brown filly is one such case.

"Everyone here in the glen knows the story of how Colin came to have her. Also, we all know him personally to be an honest, truthful man. We have all been witness to the strange power that was on the filly. We all know that she vanished utterly the moment Ian performed the one action which could break that power. And now we know that a child who went missing from her home a year ago has appeared mysteriously again at the exact time the filly vanished. Therefore—"

The minister paused to give Colin and Anna a long and solemn look. They stared back, their faces every bit as solemn as his own. Anna's mouth was half-open with wonder, and Colin felt her hand reaching out to grip his own.

"Therefore," the minister repeated, "what conclusion are we to draw from all this?"

"The same conclusion as everyone else in the glen will draw," Colin answered. "And speaking for myself, I have no doubt it is the right one. The little brown filly must have been Flora Mackenzie, and it must have been on the night of the fire that the fairies stole her and enchanted her into that shape."

"Exactly!" cried the minister. "Even if that is not the true explanation of the mystery—and I am not saying I agree with you on it, Colin—that is still what everyone will say. And what kind of life would that poor girl have then, with everybody staring at her and whispering behind her back of the strange thing that had happened to her? How could she learn to forget the tragedy of that fire that started it all? And when she grows to woman's age, what young man of the glen would marry her with such a story to her name?"

"It's a problem," Colin admitted. "And I can certainly see that the best thing would be to get her as far away from here as possible."

"Minister," Anna said suddenly, "where is the girl now?"

"Only yards from your door," the minister answered. "I brought her with me in the hope that you might agree to take her; and she is sitting out there now in the pony carriage, waiting for me."

"Call her in," said Anna, giving Colin a frown that told him to keep quiet meantime. "I want a look at her."

"I'll call her," the minister answered, "just so long as you promise to say nothing to upset her."

"I'm a mother of three," Anna told him tartly. "Don't tell me how to handle a child that's been frightened!"

"No offence, I'm sure," the minister apologised, although he could not help feeling amused at the hurt dignity in Anna's voice. He hid this feeling, however, for fear of upsetting her even further, and went to open the door so that they could all see the pony carriage standing outside it. There was someone sitting in the carriage, a small figure huddled down in the passenger seat and wearing a cloak with a hood that hid its face. The minister called out to it.

"Flora," he called. "I want you here a moment."

The hooded face turned uncertainly towards him. He called again and the small figure rose to clamber down from the carriage. Slowly it came up the path to the door, hesitated there for a moment, and then came even more slowly into the kitchen.

"There's a good lass," the minister said kindly. Then, with careful hands, he pushed back the hood of the cloak to show the face of Flora Mackenzie. A bonnie face it was, too, with big brown eyes that had a gentle look to them, and long, soft brown hair falling around it.

"*Brown is her hair, and brown her eyes . . .*" thought Colin to himself, catching his breath in amazement at the sight of it. Anna, too, gave a little gasp of wonder, and the thought that ran through her mind was, "*Ian's lass . . . It's Ian's lass!*" The minister shot a warning look at them both, and then to Flora he said,

"No one's going to speak of what's past, Flora. But Mr and Mrs Grant, here, think that maybe they already know you. Is that so, my lamb?"

Flora gave no answer to this, except a nod. The other three all waited for the moment she would speak, but when she did so at last, she had only two words for them.

"Where's Ian?" she asked.

"Ian?" Colin repeated, and glanced out of the window that had given the minister a view of Ian coming down the hill. "Ian's not far, lass. That's him coming down the hill now, in fact."

"I want to see him," said Flora then, and Colin told her,

"Well, that's soon arranged!"

With this, he opened the window and gave a long shrill whistle that made Ian quicken his steps and then break into a run. Flora turned her face towards the door, and waited with her eyes fixed on it. The others waited too, none of them saying a word, and it seemed to Colin that the silence in the room was so alive with this feeling of waiting that he could have put out a hand to touch it, as if it had been a real thing. Then the sound of Ian's running steps broke into the stillness. The steps pounded up the path. The door was pushed open, and Ian was standing there staring straight at Flora.

For a moment—just for a moment—his eyes were puzzled. "I know you," said he, "but—"

The puzzlement in his eyes changed to a look of wonder, and this grew into a delight that was touching to see.

"You've come back!" he exclaimed. "You've come back at last!"

"Yes," said Flora, and smiled, a smile that began slowly and grew until her whole face glowed with it.

"I've seen you up there in the clearing—quite a few times," she went on. "But I always ran away before you could speak to me."

"You shouldn't have done that," Ian told her. "I was searching for you."

"I hoped you were," Flora answered. "That was why I kept going back to the clearing, but I—I was always—"

She hesitated, looking away from him with a blush coming up over her face; and seeing this, Ian guessed,

"Too shy to speak?"

Flora nodded, then turned her face to him again. Upon which, the two of them stood beaming at one another as if there was not another soul in the world but themselves and all heaven and earth was theirs to command.

"Ian!" Anna said briskly breaking into the spell of this moment. "Your father and I have business to talk over with the minister, and so we want you to take the lassie off with you and look after her for a wee while."

"Yes, Mam," Ian answered. And still never taking his eyes off Flora, he held out a hand. Flora placed her hand in the one he offered. Ian drew her out the door with him, and away towards the hill. Side by side they wandered slowly up the slope of the hill, their hands still clasped, their faces turned towards one another as if they were talking nineteen to the dozen of all the things they had been saving for that moment of meeting again. The other three watched them from the window, with the minister exclaiming,

"Did you see how Flora smiled when she saw him? Did you

see her? And that was the girl I thought would never smile again!"

Colin and Anna shook their heads in wonder over this, and then Colin said,

"I can see something else too, now." He nudged Anna, and went on, "Do you notice it, Anna—the neat, light step that girl has?"

"Aye, I've noticed," Anna told him. "It's the very same step the filly had—so neat and delicate she was like a dancer moving."

"And see there—there's something else you'll remember as well as I do," said Colin, giving her another nudge; because Ian, by this time, had begun stooping to pick some of the flowers thrusting above the grass of the hill. Long trails of purple vetch, he picked, red and yellow spikes of the starry-flowered St John's Wort, and tall stems of the great golden-eyed daisies they call "gowans".

When his hands were full of these, he gave them to Flora to hold while he wound some of the gowans into a crown for her head. Carefully, when this was finished, he placed it in position, and she walked on with him, with the gowans gleaming gold and white against the brown of her hair . . .

"*. . . like a princess,*" thought Colin, and remembered how this very thought had occurred to him when he had seen Ian come home with the filly wearing her crown of flowers. But as it had turned out, of course, the filly had not been truly a princess after all. She had just been an ordinary girl unlucky enough to have fallen under a fairy spell, and it was only Ian's imagination that had made her seem like a princess. As it was doing still, for Flora . . .

With the sudden feeling that he and the others were prying too far into matters that both Ian and Flora would rather have private to themselves, Colin turned away from the window. Anna and the minister followed this example, and as they all took their seats again, Colin said,

"I'll tell you something, minister. You'll remember how everyone in the glen used to call the little brown filly 'Ian's lass'; and anyone with eyes to see or ears to hear would realise that, the moment he saw Flora, he knew he had found his lass again."

Anna nodded her agreement to this, and Colin went on, "Well now, minister, you may still be thinking that Flora could not have been enchanted into the shape of that filly. But if Ian does not doubt this, then neither should you, because these two had truly given their hearts to one another; and however wrong others may be in such cases, there can be no mistake made by true heart meeting again with true heart."

"That could be so, Colin," said the minister. "That could be so. But I've already told you that a man in my position has a duty not to encourage talk of uncanny matters such as the one that lies behind all this. And so, whatever I may think, we had better speak no more of what is past for young Flora, but look to her future instead."

"I can tell you her future," Anna announced. "She is going to America with us."

"Indeed!" exclaimed Colin, rounding on Anna before the minister could speak. "You're quick to make decisions, aren't you? But who gave *you* the right to wear the breeches in this house?"

Now Anna Grant had always been a good mother to her three sons, but—like most other women—she had always wanted a daughter also. Indeed, fond as she was of her menfolk, there were times when she was furiously annoyed with all of them for treating her as unreasonable simply because she took a woman's view of something, instead of a man's view. She would grow sick and tired then of being the only woman in the house and would have given anything for a bit of feminine company.

That was when her secret longing for a daughter always used to come to the surface of her mind; and that was always also the time when she realised all the other pleasures she had missed through not having a daughter. She could just see herself now, having all these pleasures through Flora—dressing one another's hair, making pretty clothes together, having their own kind of secrets that the menfolk would never understand anyway; and so now she faced up to Colin with a fury that surprised him.

"And what makes *you* so sure you're cock of the walk?" she flared. "There's been many a time before this when you were away in the forest, and there was no one here *but* me to take the decisions. You were glad enough then to let me wear the breeches, weren't you? And so what gives you the right to talk so high-and-mighty now about this decision?"

"Aye, aye," said Colin, backing down from this tirade. "Aye, aye, minister. It seems I'm not the only one here that can fly into a temper!"

"Oh," said the minister tactfully, "I'm sure Anna has her reasons for deciding you should take Flora with you. And if we ask her nicely, I'm sure she'll tell us what these are."

This was enough to soothe Anna's ruffled feathers; and speaking quite peaceably now, she went on,

"It's quite simple, minister. We can all see plainly that the girl will always be a wonder and a curiosity to the rest of the glen folk, but she would have a new life with us in a country where no one would know of this business. As for myself, I want a daughter. I always have longed for a daughter, and I would find peace for that longing in Flora."

The minister looked at Colin, who said plaintively, "Well, now that I am allowed to speak in my own house, I might as well tell you that Ian is the one I'm thinking of in all this. He's a fine lad, is Ian, but he's never had the chance of play a young one should have. He's a boy that uses his imagination too, and so he needs to talk, but he never did have anyone to talk to until he had the little brown filly. And now that she's gone and Flora has appeared instead—well, it would be just plain cruelty to separate them again. And that's why *I've* decided we should take Flora to America with us."

The minister drew a great breath of satisfaction. "Well, whatever the reasons for it," said he, "it's a decision that completely solves the girl's problem. And since it also solves my problem of what to do with her, I've a duty to see you don't lose by it."

With that, he took the money for Flora's fare from his pocket, and laid it on the table. "You'll find there's enough there," said he, "to pay for Flora's passage to America. And my thanks to you both goes with it now."

He put on his hat then, and prepared to leave; but Colin was up before him, meaning to pour the parting drink that Highlanders call "a drink at the door"—*deoch an doris*, to give it the Gaelic name they would use.

"You'll take a dram, minister?" he asked, reaching for a bottle and some glasses.

The minister frowned a little. "Well," said he, "not in the ordinary way of things, as you well know, Colin."

"I do know," Colin admitted. "But this is no ordinary day for any of us."

"To be sure, to be sure," the minister agreed, the frown lifting and a smile coming instead. "Besides which, Colin, *deoch an doris* is a very old custom—"

"Man, you're right at that," interrupted Colin, busy now at filling the glasses.

"And I would not feel at ease in refusing to share it with you at such a time," the minister went on, taking the glass Colin offered him. "To yourselves and Flora in the new life," said he then, raising his glass.

"Amen to that," Colin and Anna replied. And so the toast was drunk.

The minister had one more parting word, however, and at the door he turned and said it. "Oh, and by the way, you'll not need to break the news of all this to Flora. I more than hoped you'd agree to take her along with you, you see. In my heart, I was certain you would—which means I've already told her she's going to America with you, and you'll be glad to hear she's looking forward to that."

With a smile and a wave then, he hurried out to his pony carriage, and while he drove briskly off in this, Colin and Anna stood trying to take in the fact that his plan for Flora had been cut and dried before they even saw him that day.

"Which was a liberty on his part—nothing less!" declared Colin angrily; and raged all the more, the more he realised how skilfully the minister had coaxed them to consent to this plan. In the end, however, he came around to the consoling and perfectly true thought that the minister's way of looking at things had really been a great compliment to himself and Anna, and she agreed with him on this.

"Although it's me that has the thick end of the stick now!" she added ruefully; and reached for her sewing-basket, meaning to start work right away on all the things she would need to make to get Flora ready to go to America with them. This was a strong hint to Colin to leave her in peace and get on with his own business, and as Colin followed this hint, a curious thought struck him.

If it had not been for the Grollican, he realised, Flora would still have been under the spell the fairies had put on her. And so, bad and spiteful as its intentions had been, this was one time at least when nothing but good had come of them in the end. Colin found himself chuckling at the thought of how much this would annoy the Grollican; and his laughter grew all the louder when he went on to imagine its rage on waking up a few mornings hence and finding himself gone—escaped for ever from its clutches!

10 Catching the Grollican

Now THERE is no point at all in describing the voyage the Grants and Flora had to make to America, because it was one that thousands of people before them had made; and all the details of such voyages have already been put down in books for anyone who happens to be interested enough to read them. The only thing of importance about *their* voyage, therefore, is the way they all felt about it, and that is soon told.

Ian and Flora enjoyed it, of course, even although the decks of the ship were crowded with people as poor as themselves, all going to seek their fortunes in America. They explored the whole ship, raced up and down ladders, played hide and seek in all the curious hiding-places a ship offers, and generally had a good time to themselves. Best of all, they had plenty of chances to talk, so that by the time the voyage was over they knew everything about one another and were as happy with that as if neither of them had ever felt what it was to be lonely —as indeed each of them had been all their lives before then.

Anna moped a bit at first because she could not help thinking of the two sons she had left behind her in the glen. Even so, however, she had good memories of parting from them, with both of them looking so big and manly as they stood waving from the door of the house, that she could see quite well it was high time they were on their own anyway. Besides which—as she told Colin later—each of them had confided to her before she left that he had an eye on a nice-looking girl with a view to marriage; and so she knew it would not be long before they were both happily settled.

Colin agreed with this, although he also felt the ache of parting from his sons. He missed his dogs, too, and many a time in his dreams he heard their howling when he left home, and wished he could have brought them with him. He never let these feelings get the better of him, however, because he was determined that nothing should spoil his triumph at escaping from the Grollican; and with every day that passed, this triumph grew all the greater.

Colin felt himself a new man, in fact, before the voyage ended. Every morning he awoke to nothing but the promise of a peaceful day. Every day, that promise came true; and for a man who had been so troubled by the Grollican, this was such a wonderfully changed state of affairs that he could hardly believe it would last. And yet it did, right throughout the voyage, which meant he had no difficulty at all in keeping his temper all that time; and long before the coast of America came into view, he was convinced that this would always be the case.

So the time finally came for going ashore at the harbour for the city of New York, and the whole family found themselves on a deck that was jam-packed with people and their luggage. There was boxes and bundles too—masses of them—and great piles of sacks full of the provisions that people had to take with them on a journey in those days.

Everything was in the greatest confusion, in fact, and what with all the pushing and shoving this caused, the Grants and Flora found it hard to stay in the one little group. Anna and Flora, indeed, finally did get separated from the other two, and as the boat drew up to the quay where they were to go ashore, Colin and Ian finished up jammed against a huge pile of goods that had a sack of flour perched right on top of it. Colin steadied Ian with the grip of one hand, steadied himself by taking hold of the sack of flour with the other, and the two of them stared down at the quay from eyes that fairly popped in wonder at all they saw there.

This was partly because they were country folk, of course, and therefore totally unused to all the traffic of a busy quay; but even if they had been city folk they would still have stared because, even in those days, New York was a very large city which was also a great and important seaport.

"The noise!" exclaimed Ian. "I never thought there could be such noise!" And truly, what with ships' sirens hooting, voices yelling, and the thunder of great horse-drawn waggons entering and leaving the warehouses on the quay—not to mention a thousand other things—this noise was something remarkable to hear.

"And the people!" added Colin, shouting to make himself heard above the din. "My cousin Hamish is sure to come to meet us here, but how will I ever find him in all that crowd?"

The side of the boat bumped gently against the wall of the quay. Lines were thrown ashore and hauled tight around a capstan to hold the boat tied. Eagerly Colin scanned all the faces below him on the quay. Anxiously he listened for the sound of his cousin's voice shouting up to him. Yet still, not a single glimpse of a known face did he have. Not one note of a friendly call did he hear. To his horror, instead, what he *did* hear above all the rest of the din was a great, harsh voice bellowing,

"*I got the boat before you, Colin!*"

And what he *did* see standing on the quayside, was the Grollican.

It was only for a couple of seconds that this sight lasted, but for Colin, it seemed much longer than that. Like a man struck paralysed he gaped at the huge grey shape with its hideous hump and three-toed feet, the bad wild eyes glaring out of its ugly face, and its four long hairy arms waving up to him. All the rage and hatred he had ever felt against the Grollican gathered in him while these two seconds lasted. And as the Grollican vanished again, all his good resolutions about keeping his temper vanished also.

He let out a roar of anger so loud that it startled even the bustle on the quay into a sudden quiet, and turned blindly to push his way off the boat. But Ian had also seen the Grollican. Ian's eyes had marked the spot where it stood, and Ian did not have anger to blind his brain. In the time it took for Colin to let out that roar of fury, he had realised the one way it would be possible to catch the Grollican and finally hold it at their mercy. He screamed this out, clinging hard to his father to stop him turning away; and in a flash, Colin also saw what could be done.

In one movement he whipped out his pocket-knife and sent the blade slashing down the sack of flour perched on the pile of goods beside them. A heave of his shoulder sent the burst flour-sack over the side of the boat and hurtling straight down to the quay.

There was a hundredweight of flour in that sack, and the Grollican had been so sure of itself that it had not budged an inch from where it stood. The burst sack struck squarely on top of its head. The whole hundredweight of flour poured down over it, every grain lodging on a hair of its grey fur, clinging there, and thus making it instantly visible to everyone as a monstrous white figure towering among them.

People screamed, and scattered from the sight. The horses pulling the goods waggons whinnied in terror, then reared up in their traces, sending loads tumbling, turning the waggons over on their sides. Ships' sirens sounded a frantic warning, and the Grollican itself took to its heels, racing along the quayside and bellowing as it ran.

The creature had realised what had happened to it by this time, of course, and since this meant it could no longer make itself invisible, it was simply looking for a place to hide. None of the folk there realised this, however—nobody in New York ever having heard of the Grollican—and so they were all in wild terror of their lives. Even strong men gave yells of alarm and leapt aside from the Grollican's path, and from everywhere came shouted pleas to fetch the police, the fire-brigade, the army—anything that would capture the monster and put an end to the chaos and the panic.

Meantime, while all this was taking place on the quay, Colin and Ian were busy fighting their way off the boat. Anna and Flora saw them at this and tried to stop them, but they were both sure of what they had to do next and neither would pay any heed to the pleadings of the women-folk. The deck of the boat was so crammed, also, that it took them a good few minutes to reach the gang-plank, and by the time they had run down this and on to the quay, the situation there had changed completely.

All the normal traffic of people on the quay had vanished, and the only figures to be seen there were policemen and firemen. The policemen were waiting around with their guns drawn. The firemen had rolled out the hoses of the two big fire-tenders they had brought, and stood ready to man these hoses. Outside the closed doors of a warehouse stood the Chief of Police with a megaphone in his hand, and it was towards the doors of this warehouse that the guns of the policemen and the hoses of the firemen were pointed.

"Get back there!" one of the policemen shouted as Colin and Ian ran along the quay. "Get back! The monster's cornered in that warehouse, and you're in our line of fire if it breaks out!"

Ian faltered in his step, but Colin whispered, "Remember I'll need you, son." And bravely, he ran on.

The Chief of Police had raised his megaphone to his lips by this time, and was shouting a message telling the Grollican to surrender.

"Come out!" he shouted. "We have you surrounded. Come out, and walk slowly, or we shoot!"

Colin panted up to the Police Chief and grabbed the hand holding the megaphone.

"That's no use," he gasped. "The creature doesn't understand what you're saying."

"Who are you?" snapped the Police Chief. "And what do you know all about this?"

"I know that the creature cornered in there comes from the Highlands of Scotland," Colin told him. "And it won't understand you because the only language it speaks is Gaelic."

The Chief looked puzzled at this. "*You* come from the same place by the sound of you," he said. "And you speak English."

"Och aye," said Colin. "Most of us in the Highlands can speak English just as well as we speak the Gaelic. But that doesn't apply to the Grollican—which is the name of the creature you have in there—because the Grollican belongs to the Otherworld, and Otherworld creatures have never had anything but Gaelic to their tongues."

If the Police Chief had been puzzled before, he was now completely mystified. "You could be talking double-Dutch so far as I'm concerned," he complained. "But what's all this leading up to anyway?"

"Just this," Colin told him. "Let me take a hold on the

nozzle of one of those fire-hoses and go into that warehouse. I'll speak to the creature then, in its own language; and once I've done so—I give you my word on this—it will vanish and cause you no more trouble."

"You're mad!" cried the Police Chief. "It would be certain death to go in there!"

The moment had come to use Ian's presence to help him, Colin realised, and boldly he seized that moment.

"Not for me, it wouldn't," he told the Police Chief. "And to prove how sure I am of that, I'll take this boy here—my youngest son—into the warehouse with me."

The Police Chief pushed back his hat and scratched his head. "You must be sure," he said, "or you wouldn't make such an offer. But what about the boy himself? Isn't *he* scared?"

"Not me!" said Ian, speaking up on his own behalf. "It won't be the first time I've faced the Grollican."

"Well," the Police Chief told Colin doubtfully, "if that's the case I've half a mind to take you up on your offer."

"You do that," Colin coaxed, "and you'll not regret it, I promise you."

"It's easy to make promises," the Police Chief answered doubtfully, "but a lot more difficult to keep them."

He was yielding, however, and Colin could see that. A bit more arguing, a bit more coaxing, and he had his way. The Police Chief spoke to the firemen, who agreed to give up one of their hoses. Colin gripped this by the nozzle, and dragging it along behind him, he advanced on the door of the warehouse. Step by step of the way, Ian went with him; and just before they pushed open the door, Colin shouted—in the Gaelic, of course,

"It's me, Colin Grant! And Ian's with me. We're coming in, Grollican!"

One big push and the door swung open. Inside the warehouse, all was dimness, but the coating of white flour betrayed the Grollican, and they saw it standing backed up against the farthest wall. The moment it saw them also, it began to roar, but Colin shouted,

"That won't do you any good, Grollican, and it doesn't frighten us!"

"Maybe not," snarled the Grollican, "but you'll be frightened enough when my mother, the Voght, turns up to get me out of this fix!"

"Rubbish!" Colin retorted. "We'll not see the Voght here this day, because now you've been stupid enough to put an ocean between you and her. And even the Voght can't cross *that* in a flash."

The Grollican raged and fumed then, but it still had no answer to this, and so it simply began roaring again; and once again, Colin shouted it down.

"Hold your tongue, you monster," he ordered. "We've caught you at last, and so you have to listen to us."

This was the whole truth of the matter, of course, because the Grollican could not become invisible so long as the white flour clung to its fur; and so long as people could see it, it could not escape. Nevertheless, it took a great deal more roaring and grumbling before the Grollican was prepared to admit this truth, and it was only then that Colin was able to hold a reasonable conversation with it.

"I'll never get rid of you, Grollican," he said then, "and that's something I'll accept now, once and for all. On the other hand, you have to admit that you no longer have the power you once had, because I have discovered how to make you visible whenever I choose—"

"That's what you think," the Grollican interrupted spitefully. "But you won't always have a sack of flour handy!"

"True," Colin agreed. "But I can always have a shotgun with me, and if I load it with a charge of chalk, that will serve just as well to scatter white all over you. And so I'll strike a bargain with you, Grollican. Instead of troubling me in the future, you'll be my servant and work hard for me—"

Once again the Grollican interrupted, with a howl of protest this time, but Colin simply went on as if it had not made a sound.

"You'll be Ian's servant too, once I'm dead and gone," said he, "and his son's servant, and his son's son's servant. And so on, for ever and ever—or at least for as long as there is one of my name living; in return for all of which, I will provide the means to let you make yourself invisible again."

"NO!" howled the Grollican. "No, no, NO!"

"Oh, yes," Colin insisted. "Yes, yes, YES!"

"But that's not a fair bargain," the Grollican protested. "*I* can't help being ugly, can I?"

"Who said you could?" asked Colin. "And anyway, what's all this got to do with your ugliness?"

"Ask him," the Grollican said sulkily, with a nod at Ian. "*He* knows."

Ian glanced from the Grollican to his father. "That's right, Da," he agreed. "The creature told me all about it, and I'm sure it was speaking the truth. It thinks that everyone hates it, just because it's so ugly, and that's why it behaves so wickedly— just to pay people out for this hatred it fancies."

"That's stupid," Colin argued. "*I* don't hate it because it's ugly. I hate it because of the way it's troubled me, and so it's got nothing to blame but itself for the fix it's in now."

"I've got you to blame too, you fool," the Grollican said rudely. "It wouldn't have amused me to trouble you if you had been able to keep your temper."

"That's true, I suppose," Colin allowed. "But you won't get so much out of me on that score now, I can tell you, because I'm becoming quite good at keeping my temper. In fact, Grollican, it's changed days for us both, and the sooner you admit that the better it will be for you."

"I'll admit nothing," the Grollican roared. "And I won't work. I won't!"

"But if you work for us," Ian suggested, "you would have company in your days. And that would be better for you, surely, than being lonely for the rest of time, the way a wicked creature like you must be?"

"What I am is my business," the Grollican told him sulkily. "And what's good for me is my business too."

This silenced Ian, for the moment at least. Yet still it seemed to him that once more he had caught a glimpse of the odd sadness that lurked behind the bad wild look in the Grollican's eyes; and he thought to himself that the sadness would not have been there unless the creature was secretly longing to believe what he had said to it.

"Anyway," Colin continued the argument, "you can't get out of your present fix without my help, Grollican, and so you've got to accept my bargain."

The Grollican shot him a look of great cunning. "First of all," it suggested, "tell me what kind of help you mean to give, and then I'll consider this bargain of yours."

"Oh no! Oh dear no!" said Colin, who had been keeping the nozzle of the firehose well hidden behind his back, all this time. "You don't think I would be so simple as to do that, do you? What's more, you'd better not count on sliding out of the bargain as soon as you're away from here, because I'll make good and sure you won't do that."

"That's what you think," the Grollican jeered again, "but

you'll never get the better of anything so cunning as me, Colin Grant."

"Yes I will," Colin insisted. "I'll not lift a finger to help you until you've sworn on the name of your mother, the Voght, that you will keep your side of the bargain."

The Grollican howled its loudest yet at these words, because —in its own peculiar way—it loved its monstrous mother. The Voght, after all, was the only creature in the Otherworld as ugly as itself. The Voght had always saved it from the worst of its own folly. And so, to break an oath sworn on her name would also be to break trust with her—which would be a final piece of wickedness even *she* would not forgive, and thus it would be cut off from her for ever!

This was something that even the Grollican could not face, but it had not counted on Colin guessing as much. It not only howled, therefore. It raged and stamped and shook all four fists at him; but it could not go further than this, of course, without wrecking its chance of escape, and all of them knew that to be so. The display of rage was simply one more effort to frighten Colin and Ian, but when they stayed calm in the face of it the Grollican had to fall silent at last, and Colin knew then that it had yielded best to him.

"Swear the oath," he ordered; and sullenly, glaring and clashing its fangs on every word, the Grollican swore on the name of the Voght that it would no longer trouble Colin, but would be a servant to him and to his descendants for the rest of their days.

"And now you keep your part of the bargain," it shouted at Colin when this ceremony was over.

"Certainly," said Colin, all smiles now; and gave a nod to Ian.

Ian darted to the door of the warehouse. From there he called out to the firemen still patiently manning the water-pumps, and they waved back to let him know they were turning on the water. Colin waited a few seconds—just long enough for the water running through the hose to reach the nozzle and make it jerk in his hand. Then he swept the nozzle from behind his back and pointed it straight at the Grollican.

A jet of water hit it full in the chest—a great, powerful jet that broke and ran in streams all over it.

"It's cold! It's cold!" howled the Grollican.

"It will wash the flour off you, all the same," shouted Colin, laughing, and played the jet up and down, up and down over every inch of its great, furry body.

Bit by bit as the flour was washed off it, the Grollican began to disappear, until all that Colin and Ian could see of it were its big feet dancing furiously about in a puddle of floury water. Colin directed the jet at these feet. The last of the flour around them was washed away and the invisible form of the Grollican rushed past him, roaring still and spraying him with water from its wet fur. Colin backed towards the door of the warehouse, shouting over his shoulder for the water to be turned off.

"Something came out of there!" the Police Chief yelled excitedly to him. "I didn't see it, but I felt it rushing past me. Look, it's made me all wet!"

"Well," said Colin, "if that's the worst the Grollican ever does to you, you're a lucky man. It's a wicked creature, you know—a real wicked one. But now it's gone from here at least, and so *you* don't need to bother any more about it."

"H'mm," the Police Chief remarked. "You seem mighty sure of that!"

"I am," returned Colin—boasting a bit by this time. "Indeed, I'm so sure of it that I'll go even further and give you my word on this. No one—and that includes myself—will ever again have to worry about the Grollican!"

11 *As Things are Now*

THERE WAS very little the Police Chief could say after that, even although he was still not sure whether or not he had seen the last of the matter. There was nothing he could do, either, except try to get the business of the quay back to normal as quickly as possible. It was not quite the end of the story for Colin, however; and so, from the moment he was free to gather his family again, this was the way of things.

His cousin Hamish, as it happened, had turned up to meet them after all; and for all that this cousin was not quite the important man he had made himself out to be in his letters home, he was certainly able and willing to put Colin in the way of getting land to farm. He gave them all house-room too, until this matter was settled, so that they had nothing to worry about in that direction either.

In a very short space of time, therefore, Colin was busy clearing his new land and building a house on it. Also, these activities went forward so fast that the neighbourhood was amazed at what one man with only a boy to help him seemed to be managing—but this, of course, was because they had no idea of the other help that Colin was getting from the Grollican.

The creature was most unwilling about this at first, mind

you. Also, in spite of its four arms, it was terribly clumsy, and much too impatient for the neat kind of job that Colin insisted it should do. Yet still it could not get out of the bargain it had made; and so, sulk and protest as it would, it still had to do as Colin said.

Just to remind it of this, too, Colin loaded his shotgun with the charge of chalk that could make it   visible again, and kept this shotgun always by his side. But even so, the amount of quarrelling that went on between them over every job had a very bad effect on his temper, and he was delighted one day when he discovered that the Grollican's tender spot was its pride in its own strength. This gave him an idea, and the next time it sulked he taunted it,

"You're just not strong enough for the work, I suppose."

"There's nothing stronger than me!" howled the Grollican, and to show how true this was, it pitched into the work in hand like a creature possessed.

After that, Colin had only to repeat his taunt for the Grollican to go at things in the same way; and soon it was working so hard and with so little protest that he suspected it was actually enjoying its efforts. What the Grollican was really enjoying, however, was the neighbourhood wonder at the result of these efforts, and a word of praise for them would have been meat and drink to it.

It took Ian to realise this at last—Ian still feeling in his heart that the creature had always secretly longed for company and kind words. Yet still Colin did not believe this was so, and the argument it caused between them was not settled until the day that Anna said,

"You know, Colin, temper and spite are just two sides of the same coin, and so there is really nothing to choose between you and the Grollican. One of you is as much to blame as the other for the trouble you've had, and no matter what kind of hold you have over the creature just now, there will never be any final peace for you until you admit that."

This was not unlike another lecture she had once given him, Colin remembered, and he had secretly resented it at the time. He had come much further towards mastering his temper since then, however; which meant he was a humbler man and therefore more willing to listen to advice.

"You could be right, I suppose," he admitted. "But remember, Anna, that doesn't make it any easier for me."

"In that case," Anna retorted, "have the grace to try to understand that it's not easy for the Grollican either. Listen to what Ian tells you about the creature; and then try finding out for yourself whether a word of praise will make it think less about its own ugliness and more about behaving itself."

There was justice in what she said Colin admitted to himself; and so, from that day forward, he began to put Anna's advice into practice. Not that he and the Grollican ever became friends as a result of it, of course. Far from that, indeed, the best that could ever be said of them was that they got on a bit better with one another. Even so, it was still because they *were* able to rub along together at last that Colin finally succeeded in completely mastering his temper. And as time went on, it was just because the Grollican had kindness shown to it that it lost some of its shame at its own ugliness, and so had less and less inclination to be wicked.

It was a state of truce between them, you might say, and this suited everyone, because the rest of the family were settling well enough into the new life.

Flora and Ian continued to be happy in one another's company. They also had plenty of neighbourhood friends; and since none of these knew of anything strange in Flora's life, there was nothing to worry about on that score. As for Anna, she was very proud of her new house, which was much bigger than the one she had left in the glen and so made her feel quite the lady herself when she entertained other neighbourhood ladies there.

Occasionally, mind you, Anna would still think with longing of that house in the glen, and the two sons who lived there. Occasionally also, when she thought of the glen, she would let slip some remark about the part the Grollican had played in building her new home, and this caused a few raised eyebrows among these same neighbourhood ladies.

Anna always managed to laugh this off, however, and when Flora and Ian got married as they had always meant to do, she soon found she had grandchildren enough to keep her from thinking at all about the Grollican, or about her past life. As it happened, too, the twins had long since changed their minds about getting married, they having discovered they were much too content in one another's company to give up their bachelor life—which meant that Anna had no need to fret, either, over having grandchildren she would never see.

There was only one snag to this whole situation, in fact, and Colin was the one was discovered it.

He was very fond of his grandchildren, was Colin; and so, naturally enough, he told them stories. To his dismay, however, when he came to tell them about the Grollican they treated this as just another of these stories and could not believe there really was such a creature. It was all a made-up tale, they argued, just like those other strange old stories their grandfather had brought with him from Scotland. How could it be otherwise, indeed, when he was such a peaceable old man and the man in the Grollican story was so fiery-tempered? And even more so, how could anyone believe in such a fantastic creature as the Grollican itself?

"You'll live to regret such talk," Colin warned them, "and then we'll see who has the last laugh in all this! Just you wait, and you'll find out for yourselves about the Grollican."

And of course they did find out, because the day of farm machinery arrived not long after that; and, tamed as the Grollican had become by then, it was still a creature of the Otherworld which has no machines of any kind in it. This caused it to take a great hatred against the tractor, and the reaper, and the binder, and every other kind of machine that was bought for the farm; and although it did not dare to show too much of its hatred while Colin was still alive, this caution did not last.

The moment Colin's days were done, it began working its spite against all the machines that were now owned by Ian; and after that, he never knew when any of them would go wrong. There was never any real damage done to them, mind you, the Grollican's wickedness having grown so much less over the years. Also, it could not risk breaking the bargain it had made with Colin; and, in its own way, it valued the odd sort of friendship it had with Ian. Thus Ian himself found he could always coax it back to a better way of behaving, and after a while he grew quite resigned to machines suddenly breaking down for no reason that anyone could discover.

"It's just the Grollican up to its tricks again," he would say with a shrug. And it was this that first made the children wonder if there might be some truth, after all, in the story their grandfather had told about it.

The more they grew, too, the more they wondered, because it was definitely the case that a broken-down machine would not start working again until Ian had spoken kindly to the Grollican. Also, they could not help beginning to notice that someone or something they could not see was doing quite a bit of work around the farm. Once Ian's days were ended, therefore, and it became the turn of his eldest son to be master of the farm, this son decided to carry on in the same way as Ian himself had done; and so far, the decision has proved a very good one.

Not that he or any of his family has ever seen the Grollican, mind you. And they are not likely to, either, considering the way the creature feels about itself. Moreover, none of them even gets an answer when they talk to it, the way Ian used to talk; but even so, all of them have still seen and heard enough to convince them it is there, and they take care to treat it with a bit of friendliness and respect. This means it has never become too much of a nuisance to them; and thus, the way things have turned out in the end, everyone—including the Grollican—is reasonably content.

It's still not wise, however, to be too sure of anything where a wicked one like the Grollican is concerned. What's more, it's not Colin Grant nor anyone else of his name who will have the last laugh of the story, because every family comes to an end at some time or another. The Grollican, on the other hand, belongs to the Otherworld whose creatures live for ever—which means it can count on seeing the last of the Grants underground some day; after which, for many and many and many a year afterwards, it will be free to do exactly as it pleases. And that, of course, gives the last laugh to the Grollican.

But there's no one would grudge it that, surely? By the time it gets the pleasure of that laugh, after all, the creature will have waited long enough for it. And most certainly, it will have worked hard enough to earn it!